FRANKENSTEIN

SILVER EDITION

MARY SHELLEY

EDITED BY
ADAPTIVE READER

CONTENTS

INTRODUCTION

Welcome to Adaptive Reader, your portal to the captivating world of literature, tailored to fit your unique reading abilities.

In today's fast-paced and diverse learning environment, we believe in the power of personalized learning experiences. That's where the concept of leveled reading comes in, and why we, at Adaptive Reader, have dedicated ourselves to offering a broad collection of classic novels at various reading levels. Our mission is to make the joy and benefits of reading accessible to everyone.

THE BENEFITS OF LEVELED TEXTS

So, what exactly is leveled reading? It's an approach that matches students with texts that align with their unique reading abilities. This ensures that every reader is challenged just the right amount - enough to grow, but not so much that they feel overwhelmed or frustrated.

For students, this means you'll engage with texts that stretch your reading skills while keeping the experience enjoyable and manageable. You'll gain confidence as you successfully comprehend each level and feel motivated to explore more challenging texts as your reading skills grow.

For teachers, Adaptive Reader provides a valuable tool to support differentiated instruction. You can assign the same novel to your entire class while ensuring each student reads a version that aligns with their reading level. This allows all students to participate in class discussions and activities, fostering a more inclusive learning environment.

For parents, Adaptive Reader offers a supportive tool to encourage your children's reading journey. As your child progresses through the different levels of a novel, they'll not only enhance their reading skills but also develop a deeper love for literature.

READING ACROSS MULTIPLE EDITIONS

All of our leveled novels include passage markers that correspond to the same content across every one of our editions. This means that passage '62' in our silver edition contains the same themes and plot elements as passage '62' in our original edition.

For teachers, this means that you can say "let's look at passage 35 together. What is the author trying to tell us here?" and all of your students will be reading the same content — but with vocabulary and syntax that's adapted to their reading level.

Our online reading tool, available at www.adaptivereader.com, gives students and teachers free access to the original text with passage markers. We encourage teachers to include close readings of the original text as part of their coursework, giving all students exposure to the rich original syntax and language of these exceptional authors.

THE POWER OF LITERATURE

At Adaptive Reader, we are committed to helping everyone experience the power of literature. So whether you're a student diving into a classic novel, a teacher looking for flexible resources, or a parent seeking ways to support your child's literacy, Adaptive Reader is here for you.

We invite you to embark on this exciting literary journey with us. Enjoy the world of stories, characters, and ideas that await you in our collection of leveled novels. Happy reading!

LETTER 1

Dear Mrs. Saville,

St. Petersburgh, December 11th, 17--.

I have some good news to share with you. There haven't been any problems at the beginning of my journey, even though you were worried. I arrived safely yesterday, and I wanted to let you know that I'm doing well and feeling more confident in the success of my mission.

I am already very far north of London. As I walk in the streets of Petersburgh, I feel a chilly breeze on my face. It makes me feel strong and happy. Can you imagine this feeling? The breeze comes from the places I'm going to, so it gives me a taste of the cold climate there. This makes me even more excited and hopeful about my plans. I can't help but imagine the North Pole as a beautiful and wonderful place, even though people say it's frozen and desolate. In my mind, it's a land of beauty and happiness. In that place, Margaret, the sun never sets. It's always shining on the horizon, giving everything a bright glow. I believe what the explorers before me have said. In that place, there is no snow or frost. The sea is calm, and we can sail to a land that's more amazing and beautiful than anywhere else on

Earth. This land may have things we've never seen before, just like the stars and planets in the undiscovered parts of the sky. What wonders can we expect in a land of eternal light? Maybe I will discover the incredible power that makes the compass points north. Maybe I will make important observations about the stars and planets that will help us understand them better. I am so curious to see this part of the world that no one has seen before. It's like a land that no one has ever walked on. These thoughts are so exciting that they outweigh any fear of danger or death. They make me want to start this long and difficult journey with the same joy a child feels when going on an adventure with friends. Even if what I imagine turns out to be wrong, you can't deny the wonderful things I will discover. I will find a way for people to travel to those faraway countries near the North Pole much faster. Right now, it takes many months. And I will uncover the secrets of the magnet, if it's possible. That can only happen if I embark on a voyage like this one.

These thoughts have calmed me down. Now I have a goal to focus on! Going on this journey has always been my favorite dream since I was young. I read with great passion about the many voyages that have been made in hopes of reaching the North Pacific Ocean through the polar seas. You might remember that our uncle Thomas had a whole library filled with books about these voyages. Those books became my inspiration, but my father had forbid my uncle from allowing me to go on one myself.

As I discovered the works of poets for the first time, my dreams of becoming a poet myself began to fade. Their beautiful words captivated me and transported me to another world. However, right at that time, I inherited my cousin's fortune, and my thoughts returned to the path I had always wanted to follow.

Six years have gone by since I made up my mind to do what I'm doing now. I started by getting used to tough conditions. I willingly went through cold, hunger, thirst, and lack of sleep. During the day, I often worked harder than the regular sailors, and at night, I studied math, the theory of medicine, and other parts of science that could be useful to someone exploring the seas. I did a great job. I have to admit, I felt pretty proud when my captain offered me the second-highest position on the ship and begged me to stay because he thought I was that valuable.

Now, dear Margaret, don't you think I deserve to accomplish something great? I could have had an easy, luxurious life. I'm about to go on a long and difficult journey where I'll need to be very strong. Not only do I have to lift the spirits of others, but sometimes I have to lift my own when everyone else is feeling low.

This is the best time to travel in Russia. They go fast on the snow in their sledges; it feels nice, and, in my opinion, much better than riding in an English stagecoach. The cold is not too bad if you wear fur clothes, which I am already wearing. There's a big difference between walking around and sitting still for hours, when you don't move and your blood could actually freeze. I don't want to risk my life on the road between St. Petersburg and Archangel.

In two weeks or three weeks, I will go to Archangel. I plan to rent a ship there, which is easy to do by paying for the owner's insurance. I will hire as many sailors as I need who are used to fishing for whales. I won't sail until June, though. And when will I come back? Oh, dear sister, I can't answer that question. If I succeed, it could be many months, maybe even years, before we see each other again. If I fail, I'll come back soon, or maybe never.

Goodbye, my dear and wonderful Margaret. I hope you are blessed by heaven, and I hope I am saved so I can show my gratitude for all your love and kindness.

With love,

R. Walton.

LETTER 2

To Mrs. Saville, England.

Archangel, March 28th, 17—.

Time seems to move very slowly here, surrounded by freezing temperatures and snow! But I have made progress towards my goal. I have found a ship and am now busy gathering my sailors. The ones I have hired so far seem trustworthy and brave.

But I have one wish that I have never been able to fulfill. And now, I feel the absence of it as a very big problem. I don't have a friend, Margaret. When I am filled with excitement and success, there will be no one to share my joy with. And if disappointment comes, no one will be there to support me. I need someone who has similar interests to approve or improve my plans. How such a friend would fix the mistakes of your poor brother! I am too eager to start and too impatient when faced with difficulties. But the bigger problem for me is that I am self-taught. Until I turned fourteen, I spent my time outdoors and only read Uncle Thomas's travel books. It was only later, when I couldn't benefit from it the most, that I real-ized I needed to learn languages other than my own. Now I am twenty-eight, but I am actually less educated than many fifteen-year-old students.

8   Well, these are pointless complaints. I won't find a friend on the vast ocean or even here in Archangel among merchants and sailors. But there are some emotions, different from the ordinary human nature, that exist even in these tough hearts. My lieutenant, for example, is brave and driven. I first met him on a whale ship. When I discovered that he was free in this city, I easily convinced him to join me in my venture.

9   The captain is a very kind and gentle person, and he is known on the ship for being gentle and fair when he gives orders. His good character and fearless bravery made me want to hire him as part of my team. I grew up alone and spent my younger years in a loving and caring environment with you, which made me dislike the usual harshness and violence on ships. I never believed it was necessary. So when I heard about a sailor who was known for treating his crew with kindness and respect, I felt lucky that he agreed to work with me.

I first heard about him in a romantic way from a lady who owes her happiness to him. Here's a brief version of his story. A few years ago, he loved a young Russian woman who wasn't very rich. He had earned a lot of money from rewards at sea, and the girl's father agreed to let them get married. But before the wedding, he saw his fiancee crying and pleading with him not to go through with it. She confessed that she loved someone else, but he was poor and her father wouldn't approve of their relationship. Our kind-hearted friend comforted her and, upon learning the name of her true love, decided to let her go. He had already bought a farm with his money, planning to spend the rest of his life there. But instead, he gave everything to his rival, including the rest of his reward money, so they could buy animals and start a farm together. And then he asked the girl's father to let her marry the man she loved. But the father refused because he felt obligated to our friend. In response, our friend left his home country and only returned when he heard that his former lover had married the man she truly loved. "What an amazing person!" you might say. And they truly are. But it's important to note that they didn't receive much education. They are very quiet and seem careless in their ways, which makes their actions even more surprising but also takes away some of the admiration and connection we might feel towards them.

10   But don't think that just because I complain a little, or because I can imagine finding some comfort in my hard work that I may never experience, that I am unsure about my decisions. Those decisions are solid, so maybe I'll be able to sail sooner than I thought. I won't take any risks though.

11   I am excited and a little scared about the adventure I am about to embark on. I can't quite explain the mix of emotions I feel. I am heading to unknown places, a land filled with mist and snow. But don't worry, I won't make any mistakes that could put me in danger, like the character in the story of the "Ancient Mariner." You might find it amusing that I mention it, but I have a secret to share. I think my strong interest in and enthusiasm for the mysteries of the ocean comes from reading the works of a imaginative modern poet. There's something inside me that I can't quite understand. I am hardworking and dedicated to my tasks, but there's also a part of me that loves the extraordinary and believes in extraordinary things. It's this part that leads me away from the ordinary and towards the untamed sea and unexplored territories I am about to discover.

12   But now let's get back to more important things. Will I see you again, after sailing across vast oceans and coming back from the farthest point south of Africa or America? I don't want to get my hopes up too high, but I can't bear to think of the opposite outcome. Please keep writing to me whenever you can: there might be times when I really need your letters to lift my spirits. I love you very much. Please remember me fondly, even if you never hear from me again.

With love,
Robert Walton.

LETTER 3

13 To Mrs. Saville, England.

My dear Sister, July 7th, 17—.

I'm writing a quick note to let you know that I'm safe and making good progress on my voyage. This letter will reach England on a ship returning from Archangel. Lucky for it, because I may not get to see our homeland for many years. But I'm feeling positive. My crew is brave and determined, not scared by the sheets of ice we see floating by. They're signs of the dangers ahead.

Nothing exciting has happened yet that I need to write about.

Goodbye, my dear Margaret. Be assured that I won't rush into danger, for both our sakes. I'll stay calm, persistent, and cautious.

14 But I will succeed. Why not? I have come this far, navigating through the vast unknown seas. Even the stars have witnessed my triumph. So why not continue over the wild yet controllable ocean? What can stop a determined and strong-willed person?

My heart is overflowing with these thoughts. But I must end here. May God bless my dear sister!

R. W.

LETTER 4

 To Mrs. Saville, England.

August 5th, 17—.

Something very strange happened to us, and I want to write it down even though you'll probably see me before you get this letter.

On Monday (July 31st), there was a lot of ice surrounding our ship, closing in on us from all sides. We didn't have much space to float on the sea. It was a bit dangerous because we were also surrounded by a thick fog. So we stayed still, hoping that the weather would change.

Around two o'clock, the fog disappeared and we saw huge, uneven fields of ice stretching out in every direction. It seemed like they went on forever. Some of my friends groaned, and I started to worry. But then something strange caught our attention and made us forget about our own situation. We saw a small carriage on a sledge, pulled by dogs, heading north about half a mile away. There was someone sitting in the carriage, who looked like a very tall person. We used our telescopes to watch the traveler quickly move away until they disappeared among the distant bumps on the ice.

 This was really surprising to us. We couldn't follow the person because the ice closed us in, and we couldn't see where he went, even though we watched closely.

About two hours later, we were free, but we stayed still all night because we didn't want to run into the big chunks of ice floating around in the dark. I took this time to rest for a few hours.

When morning came and it was light outside, I went on the deck and saw the sailors talking to someone in the water. It was a sled, like the one we saw before, that had drifted toward us during the night, on a big piece of ice. Only one dog was alive, but there was a person inside. He was from Europe. When the captain saw me, he said, "This is our captain, and he won't let you die in the open sea."

When the stranger saw me, he spoke to me in English, but with a different accent. "Before I come on your ship," he said, "can you please tell me where you're going?"

You may wonder how surprised I was when a man, who was in danger and had no other options, asked me where our ship was headed. I thought that anyone in his situation would consider my ship a lifeline and wouldn't want anything else in the world. Still, I answered him honestly, saying that we were exploring the northern part of the world.

When he heard my response, he seemed satisfied and agreed to come onto our ship. Oh, Margaret, if only you could have seen the condition this man was in. Gradually, he regained strength, and we wrapped him in blankets and placed him near the kitchen stove to warm up. Slowly, he started to recover and ate some soup, which made a remarkable difference in his well-being.

Two days went by like this before he could speak. I worried that his suffering had taken away his ability to understand. When he started to get better, I brought him to my cabin and took care of him whenever I could. He was a fascinating person to observe. I had a hard time stopping the crew from bombarding him with questions. But I didn't want him to be bothered by their curiosity when his body and mind needed peace and quiet to heal. However, one time the lieutenant asked why he had come so far on the ice in such a strange vehicle.

Instantly, his face became incredibly sad, and he replied, "To find someone who ran away from me."

"And did the person you were chasing travel the same way?"

"Yes."

"Then I think we saw him. The day before we found you, we saw some dogs pulling a sled with a man on it across the ice."

This caught the stranger's attention, and he asked a lot of questions about the path the "demon," as he called him, had taken. Later, when we were alone, he said, "I'm sure I've piqued your curiosity, as well as that of these kind people, but you're too polite to ask."

"Of course, it would be rude and unkind of me to pry."

"And yet, you saved me from a strange and dangerous situation; you kindly brought me back to life."

After that, he asked if I thought the other sled had been destroyed when the ice broke. I told him I couldn't be certain because the ice didn't break until nearly midnight, and the traveler might have reached safety before that time. But I couldn't say for sure.

Since then, the stranger has shown a new energy for life. He's eager to be on deck, watching for the sled that appeared before. But I convinced him to stay in the cabin because he's still too weak for the cold outside. I promised that someone would keep watch for him and let him know immediately if anything new came into sight.

Here is what has happened so far with this strange event. The stranger's health has been getting better, but he doesn't talk much and seems worried when anyone other than me comes into his room. However, he is very friendly and kind-hearted. I feel sympathy and compassion for him because he is always sad. He must have been an impressive person in the past, and even now, despite being in ruins, he is still charming and likable.

I previously mentioned, my dear Margaret, that I wouldn't find a friend in the vast ocean. However, I have found a man who I would have been happy to call my brother.

I will continue to write about the stranger in my journal whenever there are new events to report.

August 13th, 17—.

My feelings of love for my guest grow stronger every day. I am both amazed and deeply sad about how much he has suffered. It breaks my heart to see such a noble person destroyed by misery. He is gentle yet wise, and his mind is well-educated. When he talks, his words are carefully chosen, but he speaks quickly and with incredible skill.

He is much better now and spends a lot of time on deck, watching for the sled that came before his. Even though he's sad, he still pays attention to what others are doing. He has talked with me about my plans, and I've told him everything honestly. He listened closely to my reasons for believing I will succeed and every detail of the steps I took to make it happen. His understanding and sympathy made me speak from my heart, expressing how much I would give up for my project. I said I would even sacrifice my money, my life, and all my hopes. I believed that one person's life or death would be a small cost for the knowledge I wanted and the power I would gain over the forces against us. As I spoke, his face grew dark and gloomy. At first, he tried to hide his feelings by covering his eyes with his hands. But I could see tears falling down. He let out a deep sigh from his heavy chest. I stopped talking. Finally, he spoke in a shaky voice, saying, "Unhappy man! Are you as crazy as I am? Have you also tasted the intoxicating drink? Listen to me—I will tell you my story, and you will refuse to drink from that cup!"

Such words, you might think, made me very curious. But the stranger was overcome by grief and needed several hours of rest and calm conversation to regain his composure.

Once he had control over his emotions, he seemed to dislike himself for being controlled by his feelings. He pushed aside his despair and started talking about me personally. He asked about my early life, and I quickly told my story. But it made me think about different things. I talked about my desire to find a friend, someone who I could connect with on a deeper level than anyone I had met before. I believed that not having this kind of friendship would make a person unhappy.

"I agree with you," said the stranger. "We are incomplete beings if we don't have someone wiser, better, and dearer than ourselves to help us become better. I once had a friend who was the best person I've ever known, so I can judge what friendship is. You still have hope and your whole life ahead of you, so you have no reason to be in despair. But me... I've lost everything and can't start again."

While he said this, his face showed a deep sadness that touched my heart. But he didn't say anything else and went back to his cabin.

Even though he feels broken and sad, he is still able to appreciate the beauty of nature. He has a double existence. He may go through hard times and be disappointed, but when he is alone, he becomes like a heavenly spirit. He has a special glow around him that keeps sadness and foolishness away.

Do you think I'm too excited when I talk about this incredible traveler? If you saw him, you wouldn't think so. I've been trying to figure out what makes him so much better than anyone else I know. I think it's because he can understand things quickly. He is also good at talking.

August 19, 17—.

Yesterday, the stranger told me, "You can see, Captain Walton, that I have experienced terrible, unimaginable misfortunes. I had once decided that I would take these hardships to the grave with me, but you have convinced me otherwise. Like me, you are on a quest for knowledge and wisdom and I believe you can find a valuable lesson in my story. This lesson might guide you if you succeed in your mission, and give you solace in case of failure. Get ready to hear about some extraordinary events."

I was really glad when he offered to tell me his story. But I didn't want him to suffer by retelling his sad experiences. I was really curious and wanted to help him if I could. I told him how I felt.

"Thank you," he said, "for caring, but it won't make a difference. My fate is almost complete. I'm just waiting for one more thing to happen, and then I can finally rest. I understand how you feel," he said, seeing that I wanted to say something. "But you're mistaken if you think anything can change what's going to happen to me. Let me share my story with you, and you'll see how it's already decided."

He told me that he would start his story the next day when I had free time. I thanked him warmly for this promise. Every night, if I'm not too busy with my duties, I will try my best to write down what he tells me. His story must be strange and distressing.

ONE

27   I WAS BORN IN GENEVA, and my family is well-respected there. My ancestors held important roles in the government, and my father also served the public with honor. Everyone who knew him respected him for his honesty and hard work. He spent most of his youth focused on the affairs of his country, and various factors delayed his marriage until later in life.

28   My father's marriage is a great example of his character, and I want to share the story with you. One of his closest friends, a merchant named Beaufort, used to be rich but ended up poor because of many problems. Beaufort moved with his daughter to Lucerne, a town where he lived in poverty and nobody knew him. My father cared deeply for Beaufort and was very sad to see him go through these hard times. My father wasted no time and immediately set out to find Beaufort, hoping to convince him to start over with his help and support.

29   Beaufort made sure to hide himself well, so it took my father ten months to find him. He was thrilled when he finally discovered where Beaufort lived. However, when he went inside, he found nothing but misery and despair. Beaufort had managed to save only

a small amount of money from his ruined life, which was enough to help him survive for a few months. During that time, he hoped to find a decent job at a merchant's house. Unfortunately, he couldn't find any work, and the more time he had to think about his situation, the more his grief grew. After three months, he became sick and couldn't do anything.

His daughter, Caroline Beaufort, took care of him with great love and tenderness. But she saw with despair that their limited money was running out quickly and they had no other way to support themselves. However, Caroline was a very strong person with a remarkable mind, and she found ways to earn a little money to barely survive. She did plain sewing and made things out of straw, using any means possible to make ends meet.

Months went by in this way. Caroline's father got sicker, so she spent more time taking care of him. They had less and less money to live on. Finally, after ten months, her father passed away while she held him in her arms. Now she was all alone and had no money. This was the hardest blow for her, and she knelt by her father's coffin, crying very hard. Just then, my father walked into the room. He was like a guardian angel to the poor girl. She trusted him to take care of her. After her father was buried, he brought her to Geneva and made sure she was safe with a relative. Two years later, my father and Caroline got married.

My parents had an age difference. My father had deep gratitude and admiration for my mothe. This made his behavior towards her very graceful and special. He always put her wishes and comfort first. He protected her like a gardener shelters a delicate flower from harsh winds, and he surrounded her with things that would bring her joy and happiness because she had a kind and gentle soul. However, her health and her spirit had been weakened by what she had been through. In the two years before they got married, my father had slowly given up his important duties. And as soon as they got married, they decided to go to Italy, which had a pleasant climate, and embark on a journey to see all the amazing things there. They hoped this change of scenery would help my mother regain her strength.

From Italy they visited Germany and France. I, their eldest child, was born at Naples, and as an infant went with them on their trips. I was their only child for several years. They loved each other deeply and showered me with endless affection. I remember my mother's gentle touches and my father's warm smile whenever he looked at me. I was their toy, their treasure, and most importantly, their child. They believed I was a gift from Heaven, entrusted to them to raise and guide towards a happy life. They were fully aware of their responsibilities and cherished the opportunity to shape my future. They taught me patience, kindness, and self-control from a very young age, guiding me with love and care. Thanks to them, my early years were filled with joy and happiness.

For a long time, I was their only concern. My mother really wanted a daughter, but I was their only child. When I was about five years old, we went on a trip beyond Italy's borders and spent a week by Lake Como. Because of their kind nature, my parents often visited the homes of the less fortunate. It wasn't just a duty for my mother; it was something she felt compelled to do. She had experienced suffering herself and wanted to help those in need. During one of our walks, we came across a very sad-looking cottage tucked away in a valley. There were several poorly dressed children huddled around it, a sign of extreme poverty. One day, when my father went to Milan, my mother and I went to visit this home. Inside, we found a hard-working peasant couple struggling to feed their five hungry children. But out of all the children, there was one who stood out to my mother. She seemed different from the others. The four dark-eyed kids were tough little wanderers, but this child was pale and delicate. Her hair was the brightest gold, even though her clothes were shabby. Her forehead was smooth and wide, her eyes were clear and blue, and her face was so full of emotion and kindness that anyone who saw her couldn't help but think she was special, like she was sent from heaven, with a heavenly glow in her every feature.

34   The peasant woman noticed how intrigued and amazed my mother was by the beautiful girl, so she eagerly shared her story. The girl wasn't her own child, but the daughter of a nobleman from Milan. Her mother, who was German, had passed away when she was born. The baby was then placed with this kind couple to be taken care of. Things were better for them back then. They had only recently gotten married, and their first child had just been born. The girl's father was an Italian who deeply cherished the glorious past of Italy. He fought tirelessly to free his country, but unfortunately, he fell victim to its weaknesses. It was unclear whether he had died or was still imprisoned in Austria. His belongings were taken by the government, leaving his child as an orphan and a beggar. She stayed with her foster parents and thrived in their simple home, standing out like a beautiful rose in a patch of dark bushes.

35   When my father came back from Milan, he found me playing with a child in the hall of our house. This child was even more beautiful than a cherub in a painting. Her looks were radiant, and she moved with such grace. We soon learned who she was. My mother asked the kind people who had been taking care of her if they would give her to us. They loved the sweet orphan, but they knew it would be unfair to keep her in poverty when there was a better life waiting for her. They spoke with the village priest, and it was decided that Elizabeth Lavenza would come to live with us. She became more than a sister.

36   Everyone loved Elizabeth. Everyone admired and cherished her so much that it made me proud and happy to share in their feelings. The night before she came to my house, my mother playfully said, "I have a pretty gift for you, Victor. You'll get it tomorrow." The next day, when my mother presented Elizabeth to me as her special gift, I took her words literally and saw Elizabeth as someone to protect, love, and care for. We called each other cousins, but that word couldn't fully capture the special relationship we had. She was more than a sister to me and would be mine forever, until death.

CHAPTER

TWO

 WE GREW UP TOGETHER. We were always in harmony, and our different personalities brought us closer. Elizabeth was calmer and more focused, but I was more passionate and had a stronger thirst for knowledge. While Elizabeth admired the beauty of everything around us, I enjoyed figuring out why things happen the way they do. The world was like a secret I wanted to unravel. I was curious, always researching and trying to understand the hidden laws of nature. The joy and excitement I felt as I discovered these secrets are some of my earliest memories.

 When my younger brother was born, seven years after me, my parents decided to stop traveling and settled down in our home country. In Geneva, we had a house, and we also had a country house called Belrive on the eastern shore of the lake, a little over a mile away from the city. We mostly lived in Belrive, and my parents lived a fairly secluded life. I always preferred to avoid big crowds and instead formed strong friendships with just a few people. I didn't really care much about my classmates in general, but I became extremely close friends with one of them. Henry Clerval was the son of a merchant from Geneva. He was a very talented and imaginative boy. He loved adventure, challenges, and even risks just for the thrill of it. He had read many books about knights and romantic stories. He used to write heroic songs and began writing many enchanting tales and stories about knights and their adventures. He even tried to get us to act in plays or dress up in costumes, pretending to be characters from the heroes of Roncesvalles, the Round Table of King Arthur, and the brave warriors who fought to save the holy land from the infidels.

39   I had a really happy childhood. My parents were always kind and understanding. They didn't control everything we did, but they gave us so many wonderful experiences. When I compared my family to others, I realized how lucky I was. It made me really grateful and made me love my parents even more.

Sometimes, I would get really angry or passionate about things. But instead of just being interested in kid stuff, I had a strong desire to learn. But not just anything. I wasn't interested in languages or governments or politics. I wanted to know the secrets of the world, whether it was the physical aspects of things or the deeper meaning behind nature and humans. My questions were focused on the metaphysical, or the mysterious secrets of the world.

40   Meanwhile, Clerval focused on the moral aspects of life. He was interested in the heroic deeds and actions of people, and he aspired to become one of tthem. Elizabeth, with her saintly soul, brought warmth and light to our peaceful home. We were all touched by her kindness, her smiles, her gentle voice, and the loving look in her eyes. Her presence softened and inspired me, preventing me from becoming too serious or rough due to my passionate nature. As for Clerval, his noble spirit remained untouched by negativity.

41   I love thinking about my childhood memories. Back then, before bad things happened, my mind was full of bright dreams of making a big difference in the world. But as time went on, my thoughts became more focused on myself and started to lose their brightness. Looking back at my early days, I realized that certain events led to

the sorrowful story that came later. Like most things, small events led to larger events.

The study of natural philosophy is what determined my destiny. In telling my story, I want to explain the things that made me love this science. When I was thirteen, my family and I went on a trip. Because the weather was bad, we had to stay inside at our inn for a day. It was there that I found a book by Cornelius Agrippa. At first, I opened it without much interest. But as I read about the ideas he was trying to prove and the incredible things he talked about, I became really excited. It was like a bright light was shining in my mind and I couldn't contain my joy. I immediately told my father about what I had discovered. However, when he casually looked at the title of the book, he said, "Oh, Cornelius Agrippa! My dear Victor, don't waste your time on this. It's not worth reading."

If my father had explained to me that the ideas in Agrippa's book were no longer believed and that there was a better and more practical system of science now, I would have stopped reading Agrippa and focused on my other studies. However, my father didn't really look at the book I was reading, so I wasn't sure if he knew what it was about. So, I kept reading it eagerly.

When I got back home, my first thing was to get all the books by this author. Even though modern scientists had done a lot of hard work and made amazing discoveries, I always felt dissatisfied after my studies. Sir Isaac Newton once said that he felt like a child collecting shells next to the vast and unexplored ocean of truth. The other scientists I knew of seemed like beginners to me, just like me.

Regular people could see the things around them and knew how to use them practically. The most knowledgeable scientists didn't know much more than that. They had started to understand some of nature's secrets, but there was still so much we didn't know.

But here were books, and here were people who knew more and had gone deeper. I trusted everything they said and became their student. My father wasn't interested in science, so I had to figure things out on my own, like a blind child trying to learn. With the help of my new teachers, I worked really hard to understand alchemy and the search for the elixir of life. But eventually, I became completely focused on the elixir. Money wasn't that important to me, but imagine the honor and glory I would have if I could cure all diseases and make people invincible!

45   I also had other visions. My favorite authors promised they could summon ghosts or devils, and I desperately wanted to see it happen. Even though my attempts always failed, I believed it was because I was inexperienced, not because my teachers were lacking in skill or honesty. So, I spent a lot of time studying outdated ideas, mixing together conflicting theories, and struggling to make sense of a jumble of knowledge. My imagination and young mind guided me through this confusing maze.

    When I was about fifteen years old, my family and I were staying in our house near Belrive. One day, we witnessed a powerful and frightening thunderstorm. The storm came from the mountains of Jura. Suddenly, I saw a burst of light coming from an old and beautiful oak tree about twenty yards away from our house. As the bright light disappeared, the oak tree was gone too, leaving only a scorched stump behind, most of it shredded into thin strips.

46   I already had some knowledge about basic electricity before this happened. At that time, we had a man who knew a lot about natural philosophy with us, and he was very excited about this incident. He started explaining a new and astonishing theory about electricity and galvanism to me. What he said made the famous thinkers I admired, like Cornelius Agrippa, Albertus Magnus, and Paracelsus, seem much less important. Unfortunately, listening to him made me lose interest in my usual studies. It felt like nothing would ever be known or understood. Everything that had once fascinated me suddenly seemed unimportant. In a strange change of mind that often happens when we're young, I immediately gave up my old interests. I decided that natural history and everything related to it were worthless and ugly. I also developed a strong dislike for a so-called science that could never truly understand the world. In this

state of mind, I turned to mathematics and the subjects related to it. I believed that they were based on solid foundations and deserved my attention.

Our souls are built in a peculiar way, and our fates can be determined by small things. It feels like my choices was guided by my guardian angel.

This was a strong effort from the force of good, but unfortunately, it did not succeed. Destiny was too powerful, and its unchangeable laws had already decided my complete and terrible downfall.

CHAPTER

THREE

⁴⁸ WHEN I TURNED SEVENTEEN, my parents decided that I should go to Ingolstadt University to continue my education. Up until then, I had been going to schools in Geneva. But my father believed it was important for me to experience different customs outside of my home country. We set an early date for my departure. However, before that day could come, the first tragedy of my life took place. It felt like a sign of the unhappiness that awaited me in the future.

⁴⁹ Elizabeth got very sick with scarlet fever and was in great danger. Many people tried to convince my mother not to take care of her. At first, she listened to us and stayed away, but when she found out that Elizabeth's life was at risk, she couldn't control her worry anymore. She took care of her and her attentive care beat the sickness. Elizabeth got better, but unfortunately, my mother got sick too. Her fever was really bad, and the doctors worried it would be the worst outcome. Even on her deathbed, my mother stayed strong and kind. She brought Elizabeth and me together and said, "My children, I always hoped that you two would be happily married. Now, your father can find comfort in that hope. Elizabeth, my dear, you have to take care of my younger children. It's hard for me to leave you all

10

behind because I have been so happy and loved. But those thoughts aren't right for me. I will try to accept death and hope to see you again in another world."

50 She died peacefully, and even in death, her face showed love. I don't need to explain how it feels when you lose someone you loved so much. It creates a void. But as time goes on and you realize that the loss is real, the pain of grief becomes more intense. But who hasn't experienced the pain of losing someone dear? I don't need to describe a sorrow that everyone has felt and will feel. My mother was gone, but we still had responsibilities to fulfill. We had to keep going and consider ourselves lucky because there was still someone we hadn't lost.

51 My plan to leave for Ingolstadt. I asked my father to give me a few more weeks. I didn't want to be away from the people who were still here, especially my dear Elizabeth, who I hoped would find some comfort.

She tried to hide her grief and be a source of comfort for all of us. She faced life head-on and took on her responsibilities with courage and passion. She focused on taking care of our uncle and cousins. She even forgot about her own sadness as she worked to make us forget ours.

Finally, the day came for me to leave. Clerval spent the last evening with us. He had tried to convince his father to let him come with me, but he didn't see any value in his son's dreams and ambitions. Henry was deeply saddened by the fact that he couldn't pursue a broader education. He didn't say much, but I could see he was determined and inspired.

52 We stayed up late. We didn't want to leave each other or say the word "Farewell!" Finally, we said it, but we pretended to go to bed, thinking that the other person was fooled. I went down to the carriage that would take me away. Clerval squeezing my hand one more time, Elizabeth asking me to write often, and giving me one final hug and attention as my childhood companion and friend.

53 I got into the carriage and I was all alone. When I go to univer-

sity, I'll have to make new friends and take care of myself. I've always been sheltered and used to the same faces, so the idea of being around strangers made me uncomfortable. Now, my wishes were coming true, and it would be foolish to have any regrets.

I had a lot of time to think about these things and more during my long and tiring journey to Ingolstadt. I got off the carriage and was taken to my own small room, where I could spend the evening however I wanted.

54   The next day, I delivered the letters I had been given and went to visit some important professors. By chance, I ended up meeting Mr. Krempe, a professor of natural philosophy. He was a strange man, but very knowledgeable in his field. He asked me a few questions about what I had learned in natural philosophy. I didn't think much of it and casually mentioned that I had studied the works of alchemists. The professor was shocked and asked if I had really wasted my time on such nonsense.

I told him that I had. Mr. Krempe became heated and said, "Every minute you spent on those books was a complete waste. You filled your mind with outdated ideas and useless names. How could you have lived in a place where nobody told you that these ideas are ancient and irrelevant? It's unbelievable that in this age of enlighten-ment and science, you still follow the teachings of people like Albertus Magnus and Paracelsus. My dear sir, you need to start your studies from scratch."

55   With those words, he moved out of the way and made a list of some books on natural philosophy that he wanted me to get. He then let me go, but not before telling me that he would start giving lectures on natural philosophy the next week. He also mentioned that another professor, Mr. Waldman, would give lectures on chem-istry on the days he didn't.

56   I went back home feeling okay, since I already didn't think much of the authors the professor didn't like. But this encounter didn't make me want to study those subjects any more. M. Krempe, the other teacher, was not very pleasant to me. I thought the modern

study of natural philosophy was useless. It used to be different when scientists pursued immortality and power. Those ideas, even if they didn't work out, were impressive. But things had changed now. The scientists seemed to only care about proving that those ideas didn't exist, which was disappointing because those were the things that got me interested in science. They wanted me to give up exciting possibilities for boring realities.

During my first few days in Ingolstadt, I spent my time getting to know the area and the people who lived there. I also remembered what M. Krempe told me about the lectures. Even though I didn't want to hear that arrogant guy speak from a pulpit, I remembered that M. Waldman was another professor mentioned by M. Krempe. I hadn't seen him yet because he was out of town.

Out of curiosity and because I had nothing else to do, I went to the lecture room where M. Waldman eventually arrived. This professor was very different from M. Krempe. He looked to be around fifty years old and had a kind expression on his face. He had some grey hairs on his temples but the rest of his hair was almost black. He was short but stood very straight, and he had the sweetest voice I had ever heard. He started his lecture by talking about the history of chemistry and the important discoveries made by different famous scientists. Then he briefly explained the current state of the science and defined some basic terms. After doing a few experiments to prepare, he ended his lecture by praising modern chemistry in a way that I will never forget.

"The old teachers of this science," he said, "made promises that were impossible to keep and accomplished nothing. The modern experts make much humbler claims. They know that metals can't be changed into something else. They delve into the secrets of nature and reveal how it operates in hidden places. They explore the heavens, discover how blood circulates, and understand the nature of the air we breathe. They have gained new and almost unlimited powers. They can control the sound of thunder, imitate earthquakes, and even create illusions of the invisible world."

Those were the words of the professor—or rather, the words of fate—spoken to destroy me. As he continued speaking, it felt like my soul was fighting. He touched upon the different aspects of my being one by one, awakening my mind to a single thought, concept, and purpose. "So much has already been accomplished," declared the soul of Frankenstein, "but I will achieve even more. Following the path that has already been paved, I will pioneer a new way, explore undiscovered abilities, and reveal to the world the deepest secrets of creation."

I couldn't sleep that night. My insides were in chaos and turmoil, and I hoped that order would come. But I had no way of making it happen. Gradually, as morning broke, sleep finally came. When I woke up, it felt like my thoughts from the previous night were just a dream. All that was left was a determination to return to my old studies and focus on a science that I believed I had a natural talent for. On the same day, I went to visit M. Waldman. He was even kinder and more friendly in private than he was in public. In his own home, he replaced the dignity he had during his lecture with warmth and kindness. I told him pretty much the same story about my past studies that I had told his colleague. He listened attentively to my little story and smiled at the names Cornelius Agrippa and Paracelsus, but there was none of the contempt that M. Krempe had shown. He said, "These were men whose tireless dedication we owe much of our knowledge to. They paved the way for us to give new names and organize the facts they helped uncover. The works of talented individuals, even if they were misguided, almost always end up benefiting humanity in the end." I listened to what he said, delivered without any pretense or arrogance. Then I asked him for advice on which books I should get.

"I'm glad," said Mr. Waldman, "to have found a student like you. If you work hard, I believe you will succeed. Chemistry is a field of science where there have been and can still be great advancements. That's why I've focused on studying it. But I haven't ignored other areas of science either. A person would not be a good chemist if they only cared about chemistry. If you want to truly become a scientist and not just a small-scale experimenter, I suggest you explore all branches of natural philosophy, including math."

After our conversation, Mr. Waldman took me to his laboratory and showed me how his machines worked. He told me what equipment I needed and promised to let me use his machines once I had advanced enough in my studies. He also gave me a list of books I had requested. With that, I said goodbye.

This day was important to me. It determined my future path.

CHAPTER

FOUR

61   FROM THAT DAY FORWARD, I focused almost completely on studying natural philosophy, especially chemistry. I eagerly read the works of modern thinkers who had written about these subjects. I attended lectures and got to know the scientists at the university. Even M. Krempe, despite his unpleasant appearance and manners, had a lot of practical knowledge to offer. But it was M. Waldman who became a true friend to me. He was kind. He made the difficult concepts easy to understand and guided me. Often, I would work in my laboratory until morning, so engrossed in my studies that I wouldn't even notice the stars fading away in the light of day.

62   As I worked so diligently, it's easy to understand that I made rapid progress. The students were amazed at my enthusiasm. Two years went by like this, during which I didn't visit Geneva at all. I was completely absorbed in making some exciting discoveries. By the end of those two years, I even made some improvements to certain chemical instruments, which gained me a lot of respect and admiration at the university. At this point, I had learned everything I could from the professors at Ingolstadt. Since staying there wasn't helping

me anymore, I wanted to go back to my friends and hometown. However, something happened that made me extend my stay.

63   One of the things which had peculiarly attracted my attention was the structure of the human body. To examine the causes of life, we must first understand death. I became acquainted with the science of anatomy, but this was not sufficient. I knew I needed to see how a body decays. In my education my father had taken the greatest precautions that my mind should be impressed with no supernatural horrors. However, now I was led to examine the cause and progress of this decay, and forced to spend days and nights in observation where I could. I saw how the fine form of man was degraded and wasted. I paused, examining and analysing all the minutiæ of causation, as exemplified in the change from life to death, and death to life, until from the midst of this darkness a sudden light broke in upon me. I could not believe that of all people, I was the one destined to discover so astonishing a secret.

64   REMEMBER, I am not recording the vision of a madman. After days and nights of incredibly hard work and fatigue, I succeeded in discovering how to make something filled with life.

The astonishment which I had at first experienced on this discovery soon gave place to delight and obsession. This discovery was so great and overwhelming, that all the steps by which I had been progressively led to it were obliterated, and I beheld only the result. What had been the study and desire of the wisest men since the creation of the world was now within my grasp. Not that, like a magic scene, it all opened upon me at once: the information I had obtained was of a nature rather to direct my endeavours so soon as I should point them towards the object of my search, than to exhibit that object already accomplished.

65   I can see your eagerness and the curiosity in your eyes, my friend. It seems like you want to know the secret that I know, but I can't share it with you directly. Please listen to the whole story patiently,

and you will understand why I'm keeping it a secret. I won't lead you down a dangerous path like I once did, where you only end up in destruction and misery. Take heed from my experience, if not from my advice, and understand the dangers of seeking too much knowledge. It's much better for a person to be content with their own town and not aim to be more than what they naturally are.

66   When I first discovered this incredible power I had, I couldn't decide how to use it. Creating a body with all its complex parts of fibers, muscles, and veins was a difficult task. At first, I wondered if I should create a being like myself, or one that was simpler. But I was so confident and excited by my initial success that I believed I could bring to life a creature as complex and amazing as a human. The materials I had didn't seem like enough for such a challenging task, but I had faith that I would eventually succeed. I knew there would be many obstacles along the way, and that my work might not turn out perfectly, but I believed that my attempts would lay the groundwork for future success. I didn't see the size and complexity of my plan as a reason to give up. With these thoughts in mind, I began to create a human being. Because the tiny details were slowing me down, I changed my original plan and decided to make the being giant, around eight feet tall. After making this decision and spending several months collecting and organizing my materials, I started my work.

67   I felt an array of emotions that pushed me forward with great force, like a strong wind, when I first experienced success. Life and death seemed like boundaries that I wanted to break through, bringing light into our dark world. I imagined creating a new species. Thinking about all of this, I believed that if I could give life to inanimate objects, maybe, over time (although I now knew it was impossible), I could revive life in bodies that had been considered dead and decaying.

68   These thoughts kept me going as I worked tirelessly on my project. I spent so much time studying that my face grew pale and my body became thin from being confined to one place. Sometimes,

when I was so close to success, I failed. But I never gave up hope. I believed that the next day or even the next hour could bring the breakthrough I needed. I had a secret that only I knew, and it was the driving force behind all of my efforts. I worked late into the night, with the moon as my only witness, tirelessly searching for the mysteries of nature. It was a terrifying and unholy process. I tampered with the graves and used living creatures to give life to inanimate clay. The memories of those moments now shake me to my core, but back then, I was consumed by an irresistible and almost frantic impulse. I was completely focused on this one goal, to the point where I felt like my soul and senses were completely lost. It was like I was in a trance, but as soon as the unnatural drive stopped, I returned to my old self. I gathered bones from graveyards and defiled the sacred secrets of the human body with my impure hands. I had a workshop in a solitary room at the top of the house, separate from all the other rooms. It was filled with the tools and materials needed for my disgusting creation. I was so obsessed with my work that my eyes bulged from their sockets as I paid attention to every little detail. I sourced materials from the dissecting room and the slaughterhouse. There were times when I couldn't stand my own actions, but my eagerness pushed me to continue, always getting closer to finishing my work.

69   The summer months passed. Nature had never looked more beautiful. And the same feelings which made me neglect the scenes around me caused me also to forget those friends who were so many miles absent, and whom I had not seen for so long a time. I knew my silence disquieted them. I well remembered the words of my father: "I know that while you are pleased with yourself, you will think of us with affection, and we shall hear regularly from you. You must pardon me if I regard any interruption in your correspondence as a proof that your other duties are equally neglected."

70   I thought my father would blame me for my neglect, but now I see he had a point. A person who is perfect should always have a calm and peaceful mind, and never let strong emotions or short-

lived desires disturb their peace. I believe this applies to the pursuit of knowledge too. If the subject you study makes you lose interest in simple pleasures that bring pure joy, then that study is wrong, meaning it's not good for the human mind. However, if everyone followed this rule and didn't let anything interfere with their love for family and peace, we would be without a great many things.

But I forgot that I'm giving life advice when the most exciting part of my story is happening, and your expressions remind me to keep going.

My father didn't scold me in his letters, but he did notice my quietness and asked about what I was doing more than before. Throughout the winter, spring, and summer, I was too absorbed in my work to pay attention to the beauty of blossoming flowers and growing leaves, which used to bring me so much joy. The leaves had already withered by the time I was nearing the end of my project. However, instead of feeling like an artist enjoying my favorite activity, I felt more like a slave toiling away in a mine or some other unpleasant job. Every night, I suffered from a slow fever and became extremely anxious. I became afraid of the toll my work had taken on me. However, I believed that once I completed my creation, exercise and fun would help me recover from the beginning stages of illness. I looked forward to both of those things.

CHAPTER

FIVE

72   IT WAS one gloomy November night when I saw the result of all my hard work. I was filled with such anxiety that it almost felt like agony. I gathered the tools needed to bring life to the lifeless object before me. It was already one in the morning, and the rain was tapping sadly against the windows. My candle was almost gone, but in the dim light, I saw the creature's dull, yellow eye open. It struggled to breathe and its limbs twitched uncontrollably.

  I cannot fully describe the mix of emotions I felt at this terrible moment, or convey how awful the creature looked. Its limbs were the right size and its facial features were meant to be beautiful. But oh, dear God! Its yellow skin barely covered the muscles and veins beneath. It had shiny, black, flowing hair and pearl-white teeth. But these supposed luxuries only made a contrasting horror with its watery eyes, almost the same color as the pale sockets they sat in, its wrinkled complexion, and straight black lips.

73   I had worked hard for nearly two years, for the sole purpose of infusing life into an inanimate body. For this I had deprived myself of rest and health. I did my best and while I slept, I was disturbed by the wildest dreams. I thought I saw Elizabeth, in the bloom of

21

health, walking in the streets of Ingolstadt. Delighted and surprised, I embraced her, but as I imprinted the first kiss on her lips, they became livid with the hue of death; her features appeared to change, and I thought that I held the corpse of my dead mother in my arms. Then, I beheld the wretch—the miserable monster whom I had created. He held up the curtain of the bed, and his eyes, if eyes they may be called, were fixed on me. His jaws opened, and he muttered. I took refuge in the courtyard belonging to the house which I inhabited; where I remained during the rest of the night, walking up and down in the greatest agitation, listening attentively, catching and fearing each sound as if it were to announce the approach of the demoniacal corpse to which I had so miserably given life.

74   Oh no! No one could endure the horror of that face. Even a mummy brought back to life would not be as terrifying as that creature. I spent the night feeling utterly miserable. Sometimes my heart beat so fast and hard that I could feel it pounding in every vein. Other times, I felt so weak and exhausted that I could barely stand. Along with this horror, I also felt a deep sense of disappointment. The dreams that used to bring me joy and comfort had now become a living nightmare. Everything changed so quickly, and I was completely overwhelmed.

     Finally, the morning arrived, gloomy and rainy. I looked out with tired and sore eyes and saw the church of Ingolstadt, with its white steeple and clock showing that it was already six o'clock. The gatekeeper opened the courtyard gates, where I found temporary refuge for the night. I stepped out into the streets, walking quickly as if trying to avoid the creature that I feared might appear at any corner. I didn't dare go back to my room, so I felt compelled to keep moving, despite the rain pouring from the dark and somber sky.

75   I kept walking like this for a while, trying to distract my mind from the heavy burden that weighed on it. I wandered through the streets without really knowing where I was or what I was doing. I was filled with fear, and my heart beat fast. I hurried along, not daring to look around me.

It felt like I was walking alone on a dark and scary road. I kept moving forward, not daring to turn my head because I knew there was a terrifying creature following close behind.

I continued like this until I reached the inn where the different buses and carriages usually stopped. I stopped there for some reason, although I couldn't explain why. I stood there for a few minutes, watching a coach coming towards me from the other end of the street. As it got closer, I realized it was the Swiss coach. It stopped right where I was standing, and when the door opened, I saw Henry Clerval inside. He saw me and immediately jumped out of the coach. "My dear Frankenstein!" he exclaimed. "I'm so glad to see you! It's lucky that you're here just as I'm getting off!"

I was filled with joy when I saw Clerval. His presence reminded me of my father, Elizabeth, and the comforting memories of home. I grabbed his hand and in that instant, all my horror and misfortune faded away. It was the first time in months that I felt calm and truly happy. I warmly welcomed my friend and we walked towards my college. Clerval talked about our friends and how lucky he was to be allowed to come to Ingolstadt. He said, "You can imagine how hard it was to convince my father that there's more to know than just book-keeping. He didn't believe me until the very end, always saying the same thing: 'I have plenty of money and food without Greek.' But eventually, his love for me overcame his resistance to learning, and he allowed me to embark on a journey of discovery in the land of knowledge."

"I'm thrilled to see you! Before anything else, please tell me how my father, brothers, and Elizabeth are doing."

"Okay, and they're very happy, just a little worried because they don't hear from you often. By the way, I want to talk to you about them too. But, my dear Frankenstein," he said, pausing and looking closely at me, "I didn't notice before how sick you look. You're so thin and pale, like you've been staying up for many nights."

"You guessed right; I've been really busy with something lately, and I haven't been getting enough rest, as you can see. But I really hope that all those activities are finally over, and I am free now."

78   I was really scared and couldn't bear to think about or even mention what happened last night. I walked quickly, and soon we reached my college. Then, I realized with a shiver that the creature I had left in my room might still be there, alive and walking around. I was afraid to see this monster, but I was even more afraid that Henry would see him. So, I asked Henry to wait at the bottom of the stairs for a few minutes while I hurried up to my room. I reached for the doorknob before I remembered to stop. I paused and felt a cold shiver run through me. I pushed the door open forcefully, like how children do when they expect a ghost on the other side. But there was nothing there. I cautiously entered the room: it was empty. My bedroom was also free from the horrifying guest. It was hard to believe that such good luck had come my way. But when I realized that my enemy had truly gone, I clapped my hands with joy and ran back to Clerval.

79   We went up to my room, and the servant brought breakfast right away; but I couldn't control myself. It wasn't just joy that I felt; my skin was tingling and my heart was beating fast. I couldn't stay still for even a second; I jumped over the chairs, clapped my hands, and laughed out loud. At first, Clerval thought I was just happy to see him, but when he looked at me closely, he saw a craziness in my eyes that he couldn't understand. My loud and uncontrolled laughter scared and surprised him.

"Victor, my dear," he cried, "what on earth is going on? Don't laugh like that. You look so unwell! What's the reason for all this?"

"Don't ask me," I cried, covering my eyes with my hands because I thought I saw the scary ghost entering the room. "He can tell you. Oh, save me! save me!" I imagined that the monster was grabbing me; I fought hard and then fell down in a fit.

Poor Clerval! I can only imagine how he must have felt. The meeting he was looking forward to with so much happiness turned into something bitter and strange. But I didn't witness his sadness because I was unconscious and didn't regain my senses for a very long time.

80 This was the start of a nervous fever that kept me in bed for many months. Henry was the only one who took care of me during that whole time. Later, I found out that he didn't want my father and Elizabeth to worry, so he kept the true extent of my illness a secret. He knew that he could take care of me better than anyone else, and he was confident in my recovery. He thought that by looking after me, he was doing something kind for them.

But the truth is, I was really sick. If it wasn't for my friend's constant care and attention, I probably wouldn't have made it. I couldn't stop seeing the monster that I had created in my mind, and I kept talking about it non-stop. At first, Henry thought it was just my imagination acting up, but the way I kept going back to the same topic made him think that something truly horrible had happened to cause my illness.

81 By slowly getting better and having setbacks that worried my friend, I gradually recovered. I remember the first time when I was able to look at things outside with some enjoyment. I noticed that the fallen leaves had disappeared, and new buds were growing on the trees by my window. It was a beautiful spring, and it helped me get better. I also started to feel happiness and love again in my heart. The darkness went away, and before long, I was as cheerful as I was before I got sick.

"Dear Clerval," I said, "you are so kind and good to me. Instead of studying this whole winter like you planned, you've been with me in my room while I was sick. How can I ever repay you? I feel so guilty for disappointing you, but I hope you can forgive me."

"You will repay me completely if you don't worry and focus on getting better as quickly as possible," Clerval replied. "And since you seem to be in good spirits, can I talk to you about something?"

I felt a little nervous. What could he be referring to? Was he talking about something I wasn't allowed to even think about?

"Don't worry," Clerval said when he noticed my change in color.

"I won't bring it up if it upsets you. But your father and cousin would be so happy to get a letter from you in your own handwriting. They don't know how sick you've been, and they're worried because you haven't written to them in a long time."

82

"Is that all, my dear Henry? How could you think that I wouldn't immediately think of my beloved friends whom I care for deeply, and who deserve all my love?"

"If you're feeling this way now, my friend, you might be happy to read a letter that has been here for a few days, addressed to you. I think it's from your cousin."

CHAPTER

SIX

83   Clerval gave me a letter. It was from my cousin Elizabeth.

"My dear Cousin,

You have been very sick, and even the letters from Henry don't make me feel better about you. You're not allowed to write or hold a pen, but I need to hear from you, Victor. It's important for us to know you're okay. I've been waiting for a letter every day, and I convinced my uncle not to come to Ingolstadt. I didn't want him to go through the difficulties and dangers of such a long trip. I wish I could have gone myself! I imagine someone old and not very caring taking care of you. They could never understand your needs like I do, your poor cousin. But that's in the past now. Clerval says that you're getting better. I really hope you can write soon to confirm this news."

84   "Get well soon and come back to us. Our home is full of love and happiness, and we all miss you so much. Your father is healthy and just wants to know that you're okay. He always has a kind smile on his face and nothing will make him worry. You would be thrilled to see how much our brother Ernest has grown! He's sixteen now and

full of energy. He dreams of being a proud Swiss and serving our country, but we can't let him go until his older brother returns. Our uncle doesn't like the idea of him joining the military far away, but Ernest doesn't enjoy studying like you did. He prefers spending time outdoors, hiking in the hills or rowing on the lake. I'm worried he might become lazy if we don't allow him to follow his chosen career path."

85   Very little has changed since you left us, except that our children have grown. The beautiful blue lake and snow-covered mountains remain the same. Our peaceful home and happy hearts are guided by unchanging rules. I keep myself busy with small tasks that bring me joy, and the sight of everyone around me being happy and kind is my reward. Only one thing has changed in our small household since you left. Do you remember when we invited Justine Moritz to join our family? Maybe you don't, so let me tell you her story briefly. Justine's mother, Madame Moritz, was a widow with four children, and Justine was the third child. Her father adored her, but her mother couldn't stand her and treated her poorly after her father's death. My aunt noticed this and convinced Justine's mother to let her live with us when Justine turned twelve. The democratic ways of our country have created simpler and happier customs than the ones found in the big monarchies nearby. This means that the different social classes aren't as separate, and the lower classes aren't as poor or looked down upon. As a result, their behavior is more polite and moral. In Geneva, being a servant doesn't mean the same thing as it does in France and England. When Justine became part of our family, she learned the responsibilities of being a servant. But here in our fortunate country, being a servant doesn't mean you're ignorant or lack dignity as a human being.

86   Justine was your favorite, and you once said that her cheerful presence could instantly brighten your mood, just like how Angelica's beauty could in a story by Ariosto. My aunt grew very fond of Justine, so she decided to give her a better education than originally planned. Justine was incredibly grateful for this kindness, though

she never explicitly expressed it. You could tell by her eyes that she admired and respected my aunt immensely. Even though Justine was lively and sometimes thoughtless, she paid close attention to every word and action from my aunt. She saw her as a role model and tried her best to speak and act like her, which still reminds me of her to this day.

When my beloved aunt passed away, everyone was too consumed by their own grief to notice poor Justine, who had taken care of her with the utmost love and concern while she was ill. Justine herself fell ill, but there were more challenges awaiting her.

One by one, Justine's siblings died, leaving only her neglected by her mother. The woman felt guilty, thinking that the deaths were a punishment for favoring some children over others. Being a Roman Catholic, she believed her confessor validated her belief. So, a few months after you left for Ingolstadt, Justine was summoned back by her remorseful mother. It was a tearful farewell from Justine as she left our home. Her appearance had changed since my aunt's passing; grief had softened her once lively demeanor and made her more gentle. However, living with her mother did not bring back her joy. The woman's repentance wavered constantly. Sometimes she begged Justine for forgiveness, but more often she accused her of causing her siblings' deaths. Constantly being blamed took a toll on Madame Moritz, and she eventually fell ill with a decline. At first, her illness made her more irritable, but now she is at eternal peace. She passed away in the early winter when the weather turned cold. Justine has returned to us, and I love her dearly. She is intelligent, kind, and very pretty. Just like I said before, she reminds me of my dear aunt with her mannerisms and expressions.

"Let me tell you about little William, my dear cousin. You would adore him if you saw him. He's really tall for his age, and his eyes are a beautiful shade of blue. His eyelashes are dark, and he has curly hair. Whenever he smiles, he gets these adorable dimples on his cheeks, and they turn pink because he's so healthy. He's had a couple of little girlfriends already, but his favorite is Louisa Biron, a cute little girl who is five years old.

Now, I'm sure you want to hear all the gossip about the people in Geneva, Victor. The lovely Miss Mansfield has gotten many visits to congratulate her on her upcoming marriage to an Englishman named John Melbourne. Her not-so-pretty sister, Manon, got married to a wealthy banker named M. Duvillard last fall. Your favorite classmate, Louis Manoir, hasn't had the best luck since Clerval left Geneva. But he's feeling better now and is said to be close to marrying a lively and pretty Frenchwoman named Madame Tavernier. She's older than Manoir and a widow, but everyone adores her.

As I write, I'm feeling more cheerful, dear cousin. But I'm starting to worry again as I finish. Please, Victor, write to us. Just one line or one word from you would mean so much. We are thankful beyond words for Henry's kindness, affection, and all his letters. Goodbye, my cousin. Take care of yourself, and please, I beg you, write!

With love,

Elizabeth Lavenza."

Geneva, March 18th, 17—.

***

"Dear Elizabeth," I said excitedly as I read her letter, "I'll write back right away to let them know I'm okay." I wrote the letter, and it made me really tired, but I was starting to get better. Two weeks later, I was strong enough to get out of bed.

One of the first things I had to do when I got better was introduce Clerval to the professors at the university. It was tough for me because of what had happened. Ever since the night everything went wrong, I developed a strong dislike for anything related to science. Just seeing a chemical instrument would bring back all the pain and discomfort I felt. Henry noticed this and got rid of all the equipment and moved me to a different room. But none of that mattered when I met with the professors. M. Waldman made it even worse by praising me for my progress in science. He didn't realize that I didn't like the subject anymore and thought I was just being modest. He kept trying to talk about it, even though it hurt me. It felt like he was showing me the very tools that would be used to cause me harm. I wanted to show my suffering, but I couldn't. Clerval, who was always good at understanding how I felt, changed the topic because he didn't know much about science. I was grateful for his understanding, but I couldn't bring myself to tell him about what had happened. I knew he would be shocked, and I didn't want to burden him with more details.

91   Mr. Krempe was not as friendly as Mr. Waldman. Because I was feeling very sensitive at that time, his harsh and blunt compliments hurt me even more than Mr. Waldman's kind approval. "Darn that guy!" he exclaimed. "I'm telling you, Mr. Clerval, he has surpassed all of us. Yes, go ahead and stare, but it's true. A young man who, just a few years ago, believed in Cornelius Agrippa as strongly as he believed in the gospel, is now the top of the class at the university. And if he's not taken down soon, we'll all be ashamed. Yes, yes," he continued, seeing the pain on my face, "Mr. Frankenstein is modest. That's a great quality in a young man. Young men should doubt themselves, you know, Mr. Clerval. I was like that when I was young, but it doesn't last long." Mr. Krempe started bragging about himself, which thankfully changed the subject from something that was bothering me.

92   Clerval didn't share my interest in science, and his studies were different from mine. He came to the university with the goal of becoming an expert in Eastern languages because he believed it would lead him to the life he wanted. Unlike Clerval, I didn't try to understand the languages on a deep level because I only wanted to enjoy them temporarily. I read to simply understand the meaning, and it was worth all the effort I put in. Their writings had a calming effect on me and brought me joy like nothing else I've read before. When you read their stories, it feels like life is all about the warmth of the sun, being in a beautiful garden filled with roses, the mixed feelings from an attractive enemy, and the burning passion in your

heart. It's completely different from the strong and heroic poems of Greece and Rome.

93   Summer was spent doing these activities, and I was supposed to return to Geneva in the fall. However, some things happened that caused delays, and before I knew it, winter had arrived with its snow-covered roads. Despite the delay, we made the most of the winter, and when spring finally came, it was worth the wait because everything looked beautiful.

May had already started, and I was anticipating a letter that would tell me when I could finally leave. But then, Henry suggested that we take a walking tour around Ingolstadt before I went on my way. It was a chance for me to say goodbye to the place I had called home for a long time. I happily agreed to his idea because I enjoyed being active, and Clerval was always my favorite companion when it came to exploring the countryside of our homeland.

94   We spent two weeks doing these walks: my health and mood had already improved, and they got even better from the fresh air, interesting things we saw, and talking with my friend. Before, studying had made me isolate myself from others and become unsocial. But Clerval brought out the kinder side of me; he reminded me how to appreciate nature and the happy energy of children. You were such a great friend! You truly loved me and tried to make me more like you. I had been so self-absorbed and narrow-minded, but your kindness and love opened up my senses and made me feel alive again. I became the same joyful person I was a few years ago, when everyone loved me and I loved them back, with no worries or sadness. Being surrounded by beautiful nature made me feel so happy. A clear sky and green fields filled me with joy. This season was truly wonderful; the flowers of spring were blooming on the bushes, and summer flowers were starting to bud. I didn't have any troubling thoughts that had bothered me the year before, despite my efforts to push them away.

95   Henry rejoiced in my happiness, and sincerely sympathised in

my feelings. He was a great companion and told many wonderful stories to keep us occupied.

We returned to our college on a Sunday afternoon: the peasants were dancing, and every one we met appeared gay and happy. My own spirits were high.

CHAPTER

SEVEN

 ON MY WAY BACK, I found a letter from my father. It said:

"Dear Victor,

I know you have been eager to receive a letter from me, telling you when you can come home. At first, I considered writing just a few lines, mentioning the day you should return. But that would be unfair to you, and I cannot bring myself to do it. My son, imagine how shocked you would be if, instead of a happy and warm welcome, you were greeted with tears and sadness. Victor, how can I tell you about the terrible things that have happened to us? I know that even though you have been away, you still care about our happiness and sadness. How can I bring myself to hurt my son who has been gone for so long? I want to prepare you for the devastating news, but I know it's impossible. I can see your eyes scanning the page, searching for the words that will deliver the awful message.

"William is dead! He was such a sweet child, always smiling and bringing warmth to my heart. He was so kind, yet so full of life. Victor, someone has taken his life away from us!

"I won't try to comfort you right now. Instead, I will simply tell you what happened."

"Last Thursday, May 7th, me, my niece, and your two brothers went for a walk in Plainpalais. The evening was warm and peaceful, so we walked farther than usual. We didn't realize it was getting dark until we couldn't find William and Ernest, who had gone ahead of us. We sat down and waited for them to come back. Ernest eventually returned and asked if we had seen his brother. He told us that he had been playing with William, who had run away to hide and didn't come back despite waiting for a long time.

This worried us, so we kept searching until it was night. Elizabeth thought that maybe William had gone back home. But he wasn't there. We went back with torches because I couldn't rest knowing that my sweet boy was lost and exposed to the cold and damp of the night. Elizabeth was also extremely worried. Around five in the morning, I found my precious boy. The night before, he was lively and healthy, but now he lay on the grass, pale and unmoving. There was a mark on his neck left by the murderer's hand."

"He was conveyed home, and the sadness that was visible in my face betrayed the secret to Elizabeth. She was very eager to see the corpse. At first I attempted to prevent her; but she persisted, and entering the room where it lay, hastily examined the neck of the victim, and clasping her hands exclaimed, 'O God! I have murdered my darling child!'

"She fainted, and was restored with extreme difficulty. When she again lived, it was only to weep and sigh. She told me, that that same evening William had teased her to let him wear a very valuable miniature that she possessed of your mother. This picture is gone, and was doubtless the temptation which urged the murderer to the deed. We have no trace of him at present, although our exertions to discover him are unremitted; but they will not restore my beloved William!

"Come, dearest Victor, you alone can help Elizabeth. She weeps continually.

"Come, Victor; let go of thoughts of revenge against the killer, and instead, approach this situation with peace and kindness, so that we can begin to heal our wounded minds. Enter the house of mourning, my friend, with love and care for those who care about you, and not with hatred for your enemies.

"Your loving and sorrowful father,

"Alphonse Frankenstein.

"Geneva, May 12th, 17——."

CLERVAL, who had been watching me closely as I read the letter, was surprised to see the sadness that took over my initial joy upon receiving news from my friends. I placed the letter on the table and covered my face with my hands.

"My dear Frankenstein," Henry exclaimed, seeing my tears and distress, "are you always going to be unhappy? What happened, my dear friend?"

I gestured for him to pick up the letter while I paced back and forth across the room, filled with great anxiety. Tears also filled Clerval's eyes as he read about the unfortunate event that happened to me.

"I can't offer you any comfort, my friend," he said, "your tragedy cannot be undone. What do you plan to do?"

"I need to go to Geneva right away. Come with me, Henry, so we can arrange for the horses."

100 During our walk, Clerval tried to offer some words of comfort; he could only express his heartfelt sympathy. "Poor William!" he said, "such a dear and lovely child. Now he rests with his angel mother! Anyone who saw him, so bright and full of joy in his youthful beauty, would weep for his untimely loss! To die in such a terrible way; to be at the mercy of a murderer's grasp! What an even greater tragedy, to destroy such pure innocence! Poor little boy! We can only find solace in the fact that his friends mourn and weep, but he is at peace. The pain is over, his suffering has come to an end forever. He lies beneath the earth, free from any pain. He is no longer

in need of our pity, for that we must reserve for those who continue to suffer."

Clerval spoke these words as we hurried through the streets; they stuck in my mind, and I remembered them later when I was alone. But as soon as the horses arrived, I quickly got into a cabriolet and said goodbye to my friend.

My trip was very sad. At first, I wanted to hurry to console and be there for my loved ones who were grieving, but as I got closer to my hometown, I slowed down. I couldn't handle all the emotions that filled my mind. I went through places that were familiar from when I was young, but I hadn't seen them in almost six years. I wondered how everything might have changed during that time! There had been one sudden and devastating change, but many small things could have slowly caused other changes that were just as important. I felt afraid and couldn't move forward because I dreaded all the unknown problems that made me shake with fear, even though I couldn't say exactly what they were.

I stayed in Lausanne for two days, feeling this way. I looked at the lake; the water was calm and peaceful. Everything around me was still and quiet, and the snowy mountains, which I thought of as "nature's palaces," hadn't changed. Slowly, the peaceful and beautiful scene helped me feel better, and I continued my journey toward Geneva.

The road followed the edge of the lake, and as I got closer to my hometown, the lake became narrower. I could see the dark sides of Jura and the bright peak of Mont Blanc more clearly. I cried like a child. "Dear mountains! My beautiful lake! How do you welcome your wanderer? Your tops are clear, the sky and lake are blue and calm. Does this mean there will be peace or is it just teasing my unhappiness?"

I'm afraid, my friend, that I might become boring by talking too much about these early happenings. However, those were days of relative happiness, and I remember them fondly. Oh, my country, my beloved country! Only someone born here can understand the joy I felt in seeing your rivers, mountains, and most of all, your beautiful lake again!

But as I got closer to home, sadness and fear took over once more. Night fell, and when I could barely see the dark mountains, I felt even more gloomy. The scene seemed like a vast and shadowy place of trouble, and I vaguely sensed that I was destined to become the most miserable person on earth. Sadly, my prediction came true, and I was only wrong about one thing: I couldn't even imagine or anticipate a tiny fraction of the pain I was meant to go through.

103   It was very dark when I reached the outskirts of Geneva. The town gates were already closed, so I had to spend the night in a village called Secheron, which was half a league away from the city. The sky was clear, and since I couldn't sleep, I decided to go visit the place where my poor William was murdered. Because I couldn't go through the town, I had to cross the lake in a boat to get to Plainpalais. During this short trip, I saw lightning creating beautiful shapes on the top of Mont Blanc. The storm seemed to be getting closer, and when I reached the shore, I climbed a small hill to watch it move. It approached quickly; the sky became cloudy, and I soon felt the rain starting to fall slowly in big drops, but it soon became more intense.

104   I got up from my seat and continued walking, even though it was getting darker and stormier by the minute. The thunder crashed loudly above my head, echoing from Salêve, the Juras, and the Alps of Savoy. Bright flashes of lightning blinded me, lighting up the lake and making it look like a huge sheet of fire. Then, for just a moment, everything became pitch black until my eyes adjusted to the darkness again. In Switzerland, storms often appear in different parts of the sky at the same time. The fiercest storm was directly north of the town, over the part of the lake between Belrive and the village of Copêt. Another storm sent faint flashes of light to Jura, while yet another made the Môle, a pointy mountain to the east of the lake, sometimes visible and sometimes hidden.

105   While I watched the storm, so beautiful yet terrific, I wandered

on quickly. This noble war in the sky elevated my spirits; I clasped my hands, and exclaimed aloud, "William, dear angel!" As I said these words, I saw in the gloom a figure which stole from behind a clump of trees near me. I stood fixed, gazing intently. I could not be mistaken. The figure passed me quickly, and I lost it in the gloom. Nothing in human shape could have destroyed that fair child. He was the murderer of my brother! I could not doubt it and was convinced of this truth. The mere presence of the idea was an irresistible proof of the fact. I thought of pursuing the devil, but it would have been in vain, for another flash discovered him to me hanging among the rocks of the nearly perpendicular ascent of Mont Salêve, a hill that bounds Plainpalais on the south. He soon reached the summit, and disappeared.

106   I remained motionless. Two years had now nearly elapsed since the night on which the monster first received life and was this his first crime? Alas! I had turned loose into the world a terrible monster who delighted in misery; had he not murdered my brother?

No one can conceive the anguish I suffered during the remainder of the night, which I spent, cold and wet, in the open air. But I did not feel the inconvenience of the weather; my imagination was busy in scenes of evil and despair. I considered the being whom I had cast among mankind, and endowed with the will and power to effect purposes of horror, such as the deed which he had now done, nearly in the light of my own vampire, my own spirit let loose from the grave, and forced to destroy all that was dear to me.

107   The sun started to rise, and I walked towards the town. The gates were open, so I hurried to my dad's house. My first thought was to find out what I knew about the killer and make sure they were chased after right away. But then I stopped to think about the story that I had to tell. A creature that I had created and given life to had met me at midnight on a dangerous mountain. I also remembered the fever I had when I made this creature, which could make my story sound like I was delirious. I knew that if someone else told me this story, I would think they were crazy. Plus, this creature was so

strange that it would be impossible to catch, even if my family believed me and tried to chase after it. And even if we did chase after it, what would be the point? Who could catch a creature that could climb up the steep sides of Mont Salêve? After thinking about all of this, I decided to keep quiet.

It was around five in the morning when I got to my father's house. I told the servants not to wake up the family and went into the library, where I usually waited for them to wake up.

108   Six years had gone by, like a distant memory, since I last said goodbye to my father before leaving for Ingolstadt. I found myself standing in the very same spot where we had embraced. My dear and respected parent! He was still with me in spirit. I looked at the painting of my mother hanging above the fireplace. It was a historical scene, painted at my father's request. It portrayed Caroline Beaufort in a deep state of sorrow, kneeling beside her father's coffin. Her clothing was simple, and her face was pale. But there was a certain grace and beauty about her that made it hard to feel sorry for her. Underneath this painting was a small picture of William, and tears welled up in my eyes as I looked at it. Just then, Ernest walked in. He had heard me arrive and hurried over to greet me. He expressed both sadness and joy at seeing me. "Welcome, my dear Victor," he said. "Oh, I wish you had come three months ago. We were all filled with so much happiness back then. You come to us now in the midst of a misery that nothing can ease. But I hope your presence will revive our father, who seems to be losing hope. And perhaps you can convince poor Elizabeth to stop blaming herself and torturing her own soul. Oh, poor William! He was our beloved little brother, our pride and joy!"

109   Tears streamed down my brother's face, and a feeling of intense pain gripped me. Before, I had only imagined the sadness of our ruined home; now it hit me like a new and equally horrifying disaster. I tried to calm Ernest down and asked for more details about our father and the person he mentioned, who happened to be our cousin.

"She needs comfort the most," Ernest said, his voice filled with sorrow. "She blames herself for my brother's death, and it torments her deeply. But since we've discovered the murderer—"

"The murderer found! My goodness! How is that possible? Who would even dare to chase after him? It's impossible; it's like trying to catch the wind or hold back a raging river with a straw. I saw him too; he was free last night!"

"I don't understand what you're saying," my brother replied, sounding astonished. "But for us, uncovering the truth has only added to our misery. No one believed it at first, and even now Elizabeth refuses to accept it, despite all the evidence. Who could believe that Justine Moritz, who was kind and loved our family so much, could suddenly commit such a terrifying, dreadful crime?"

"Justine Moritz! Poor, poor girl. Is she the one accused? But it's unjust; everyone knows that. Surely, Ernest, nobody believes it?"

"No one believed it at first, but then some things came to light that almost made us believe it. And Justine's actions have been so confused that it adds more evidence to make us think she's guilty. Unfortunately, she's going to be tried today, and you'll find out everything then."

He told me that on the morning when they discovered poor William's murder, Justine had gotten sick and stayed in bed for several days. During that time, one of the servants found a picture of my mother in the clothes Justine had worn on the night of the murder. They thought this was the thing that tempted the murderer. The servant showed it to another servant without telling the family, and that servant went to a magistrate. Based on their statements, Justine was arrested. When she was accused, she acted really confused, which made people even more suspicious.

It was a strange story, but it didn't make me doubt. I said firmly, "You're all wrong. I know who the murderer is. Justine, poor and kind Justine, is innocent."

At that moment, my father walked in. I saw that he looked really sad, but he tried to greet me with a happy face. After we said our sad hellos, he wanted to talk about something else other than our terrible situation. But before he could, Ernest blurted out, "Oh my goodness, Dad! Victor says he knows who killed poor William."

"We know too, sadly," my father replied. "I would much rather have never known and not discovered such evil and ungratefulness in someone I admired so much."

"Dad, you're mistaken. Justine is innocent," I said.

"If she is, I hope and pray that she won't be punished as if she were guilty. She will be tried today, and I truly hope she will be found not guilty," my father said.

I felt better hearing my father's words. I strongly believed that Justine, and every person for that matter, was not guilty of this murder. So, I wasn't scared that any evidence would be strong enough to prove she did it. The story I had to tell wasn't something I could share with everyone; it was too horrifying for most people to understand. Would anyone, other than me, the creator, believe in the existence of the terrifying result of my arrogance and ignorance that I had set loose upon the world?

112 We were soon joined by Elizabeth. Time had changed her since I last saw her; it had made her even more beautiful than when she was a child. She still had her honesty and energy, but now there was an added expression of sensitivity and intelligence. She welcomed me with a lot of love. "Your arrival, my dear cousin," she said, "gives me hope. Maybe you can find a way to prove that Justine is innocent. But who is safe if she is found guilty of a crime? I believe in her innocence just as strongly as I believe in my own. Our misfortune is very hard on us; we not only lost our precious little boy, but this poor girl who I truly love is going to be taken away for an even worse fate. If she is condemned, I will never find joy again. But I know she won't be, I'm sure of it. And then I will be happy again, even after the sad death of my little William."

"She is innocent, my Elizabeth," I said, "and we will prove it. Don't worry, let your spirits be lifted by the knowledge that she will be acquitted."

"You are so kind and generous! Everyone else believes she is guilty, and that made me miserable because I knew it was impossible. Seeing everyone else prejudiced like that made me lose hope and feel despair." She cried.

"My dear niece," said my father, "stop crying. If she is indeed innocent, trust in the fairness of our laws and in my determination to prevent any hint of bias."

CHAPTER

EIGHT

113   WE WAITED SADLY for a few hours until eleven o'clock, when the trial was supposed to start. Since my father and the rest of the family had to be there as witnesses, I went with them to the court. The whole trial was a terrible mockery of justice, and it tortured me to witness it. The fate of two lives rested on this decision: an innocent and joyful baby, and a girl named Justine who had a lot of good qualities and a promising future. But now, everything was going to be taken away from her in a shameful way, and I was the one responsible. I would have rather admitted to being guilty of the crime Justine was accused of, even though I wasn't there when it happened. But if I made such a confession, people would think I was insane and it wouldn't clear her name.

114   The appearance of Justine was calm. She was dressed in all black and her face, always engaging was sincere, but beautiful. She was both steady and constant, which is likely what those looking on did not expect to see. When she entered the court, she threw her eyes round it, and quickly discovered where we were seated. A tear seemed to dim her eye when she saw us; but she quickly recovered

herself, and a look of sorrowful affection seemed to attest her utter guiltlessness.

115 The trial started. The person arguing against Justine explained the accusation, and then they called several witnesses to testify. There were some strange facts that seemed to be against her, but I had proof of her innocence, so they didn't worry me as much. They said she had been outside the entire night that the murder happened, and someone saw her near the place where they found the child's body in the morning. The person asked her what she was doing there, but she looked strange and gave a confusing answer. She came back to the house at around eight o'clock, and when someone asked where she had been all night, she said she was looking for the child and desperately asked if they had heard anything about him. When they showed her the body, she had a strong reaction and became hysterical. She stayed in bed for several days. Then they showed a picture that the servant found in her pocket. Elizabeth, speaking with a trembling voice, confirmed that it was the same picture that she had put around the child's neck just an hour before he went missing. The court was filled with horror and anger.

Finally, it was Justine's turn to defend herself. As the trial went on, her face changed. She looked surprised, horrified, and miserable. Sometimes she tried to hold back her tears, but when she was asked to speak, she gathered herself and spoke with a voice that could be heard, though it changed in strength.

116 "God knows," she said, "how completely innocent I am. But I understand that just saying I'm innocent isn't enough to prove it. I am relying on giving a clear and simple explanation of the facts that have been said against me, and I hope that my good reputation will lead the judges to see things in a positive way when something seems uncertain or suspicious."

117 She then related that, by the permission of Elizabeth, she had stayed at the house of an aunt at Chêne, a village situated at about a league from Geneva. On her return, at about nine o'clock, she met a

man, who asked her if she had seen any thing of the child who was lost. She was alarmed by this account, and passed several hours in looking for him. She was forced to remain several hours of the night in a barn belonging to a cottage, being unwilling to call up the inhabitants, to whom she was well known. Most of the night she spent here watching. It was dawn, and she thought she might find my brother. If she had gone near the spot where his body lay, it was without her knowledge. That she had been confused when questioned by the market-woman was not surprising, since she had passed a sleepless night, and the fate of poor William was yet uncertain. Concerning the picture she had no memory.

118   "I understand," said the sad person, "that this one thing makes me look really guilty, but I can't explain it. When I say I have no idea how it got there, all I can do is guess how it could have ended up in my pocket. But even then, I can't be sure. I don't think I have any enemies, and even if I did, I can't imagine why they would do something so cruel to harm me. Could the murderer have put it there? I don't know how they would have had the chance, and even if they did, why would they steal the jewel just to get rid of it quickly?

"I trust the judges to give me a fair trial, but I don't see much hope. I would like to have a few people who know me testify about my good character. But if their words don't outweigh the belief that I'm guilty, I'll be convicted, even though I know I'm innocent."

Several witnesses who had known her for a long time were called, and they spoke positively about her. However, because they were afraid and hated the crime they thought she had committed, they were too scared to come forward. Elizabeth saw her last hope, her good qualities and blameless behavior, about to disappear. Despite feeling very upset, she asked if she could speak to the court.

119   "I am," she said, "the cousin of the unhappy child who was killed, or rather his sister, because I was raised by his parents and have lived with them even before he was born. Some might consider it inappropriate for me to speak up in this situation, but when I see a person about to be harmed because of the cowardice of their

supposed friends, I want to be able to speak and share what I know about their character. I know the accused very well. We lived in the same house together, once for five years, and another time for almost two years. Throughout that time, she seemed to me like the most kind and caring person. She took care of my aunt, Madame Frankenstein, with great love and dedication during her last sickness. And later on, she also took care of her own mother during a long illness, impressing everyone who knew her with her devotion. After that, she lived in my uncle's house where she was loved by the whole family. She was deeply attached to the child who has now passed away and treated him like a loving mother. Personally, I have no doubt in saying that, despite all the evidence against her, I believe in her complete innocence. She had no reason to do such a thing. And as for the little trinket that is the main proof against her, if she had really wanted it, I would have gladly given it to her because that's how much I respect and value her."

120   A murmur of approval followed Elizabeth's sincere and powerful plea. But people were only happy with her intervention, not on the side of poor Justine, who faced renewed anger from the public. They accused her of the worst kind of betrayal. Justine cried as Elizabeth spoke, but she didn't say anything. I was extremely agitated and anguished throughout the entire trial. I believed in her innocence; I knew it. Could the monster who (I had no doubt) murdered my brother also have betrayed the innocent to death and shame for its own cruel amusement? I couldn't bear the horror of it all. When I saw that the public and the judges had already condemned my poor victim, I ran out of the courtroom in agony. The suffering of the accused was not as intense as mine. She had innocence to sustain her, but I was consumed by remorse. The torment wouldn't let go of me.

I spent a night full of pure misery. When morning came, I went to the court. My lips and throat were dry. I couldn't bring myself to ask the dreaded question, but I was recognized, and the officer understood why I was there. The ballots had been cast. They were all black, and Justine was sentenced to death.

121   I can't fully express the feelings I had at that moment. In the past, I had felt horror, and I tried my best to put those feelings into words. But there are no words to describe the overwhelming despair I felt then. The person I spoke to added that Justine had already admitted her guilt. He said that this evidence wasn't really necessary because the case was so clear, but he was glad it was there. Our judges don't like to convict someone based only on circumstantial evidence, no matter how convincing it may be.

This news was strange and unexpected. What could it mean? Was I seeing things? Was I really as crazy as people would think if I told them what I suspected? I hurried home, and Elizabeth asked me eagerly for the outcome.

"It turned out how you probably expected," I replied. "The judges would rather see ten innocent people suffer than let one guilty person go free. But Justine confessed."

This was a terrible blow to poor Elizabeth, who had strongly believed in Justine's innocence. "Oh no!" she cried. "How can I ever trust in the goodness of people again? Justine, who I loved and considered like a sister, how could she pretend to be innocent and then betray us all? Her kind eyes never showed any sign of harshness or deceit, and yet she committed murder."

122   Not long after, we heard that the poor victim had expressed a wish to see my cousin. My father didn't want her to go, but he said it was up to her to decide. "Yes," Elizabeth said, "I'll go, even though she's guilty. And you, Victor, you'll come with me. I can't go alone." The thought of this visit tormented me, but I couldn't say no.

We walked into the dark prison room and saw Justine sitting on some straw in the corner. Her hands were chained, and she had her head resting on her knees. When she saw us come in, she stood up. Once we were alone with her, she threw herself at Elizabeth's feet, crying uncontrollably. My cousin cried too.

"Oh, Justine!" Elizabeth said, "Why did you take away my last hope? I believed in your innocence, and even though I was unhappy at the time, I wasn't as miserable as I am now."

"And do you also believe that I'm so, so wicked? Are you also joining my enemies to destroy me, to condemn me as a murderer?" She could hardly speak through her sobs.

"Get up, poor girl," Elizabeth said, "Why are you kneeling if you're innocent? I'm not one of your enemies. I believed you were innocent, even with all the evidence against you, until I heard that you had confessed. You say that report is false, and let me tell you, dear Justine, nothing can make me doubt you for even a moment, except your own confession."

"I did admit to a lie. I admitted it to seek forgiveness, but now that falsehood weighs on my heart even more than my other sins. May God forgive me! Ever since I was condemned, my confessor has constantly harassed me; he threatened and scared me, making me believe that I was the monster he said I was. He threatened to excommunicate me and send me to hell if I didn't change my mind. Dear lady, I had no one to support me; everyone saw me as a wretched person destined for shame and destruction. What could I do? In a moment of weakness, I told a lie, and now I am truly miserable."

She paused, crying, and then continued, "I was terrified at the thought that you, my dear lady, would believe that Justine, whom your kind aunt had honored and whom you loved, was capable of a crime that only the devil himself could commit. Dear William! My dearest, blessed child! I'll see you again soon in heaven, where we'll all be happy. That gives me comfort even though I'm about to suffer shame and death."

"Oh, Justine! Please forgive me for doubting you, even if it was only for a moment. Why did you confess? But don't worry, dear girl. Don't be afraid. I'll declare your innocence, and I'll prove it. I'll soften the hearts of your enemies with my tears and prayers. You won't die! You, my friend, my companion, my sister, won't perish on the scaffold! No! I could never survive such a terrible tragedy."

124 Justine sadly shook her head. "I'm not afraid to die now," she said. "I have found strength in God, and He gives me courage to face the worst. I'm leaving behind a sad and harsh world. If you remember me and think of me as someone wrongly accused, I accept the fate that awaits me. Learn from me, dear lady, to patiently accept what Heaven has planned for us."

During their conversation, I had retreated to a corner of the prison room to hide my intense anguish. Despair! Who could dare speak of such a thing? The poor victim, who would pass the dreadful boundary between life and death the next day, did not feel the same deep and bitter agony that consumed me. I clenched my teeth and groaned from the depths of my soul. Justine was startled. She approached me and said, "Dear sir, you are very kind to visit me. I hope you don't believe I am guilty?"

I couldn't answer. "No, Justine," Elizabeth interrupted. "He is more convinced of your innocence than I was. Even after he heard that you confessed, he didn't believe it."

"I truly thank him. In these final moments, I have the deepest gratitude for those who think of me kindly. The affection of others is so sweet to someone like me, who has been through so much. It eases more than half of my sorrow. Now that you, dear lady, and your cousin believe in my innocence, I feel as though I can peacefully embrace death."

125 Thus the poor sufferer tried to comfort others and herself. She gained what she desired. But I, the true murderer, felt the never-dying worm alive in my bosom, which gave no hope or comfort. Elizabeth also wept, and was unhappy, but her's also was the misery of innocence. I was heartbroken. I had a hell within me, which nothing could get rid of. We stayed several hours with Justine; and it was with great difficulty that Elizabeth could tear herself away. "I wish," cried she, "that I were to die with you; I cannot live in this world of misery."

Justine assumed an air of cheerfulness, while she with difficulty repressed her bitter tears. She embraced Elizabeth, and said, in a voice of half-suppressed emotion, "Farewell, sweet lady, dearest Elizabeth, my beloved and only friend; may Heaven, in its bounty, bless and preserve you; may this be the last misfortune that you will ever suffer! Live, and be happy, and make others so."

126 And the next day, Justine died. Elizabeth's heartbreaking words failed to persuade the judges to change their minds about the innocent sufferer being guilty. My passionate and angry pleas fell on deaf ears. When I heard their cold responses and listened to the heartless reasoning of these men, I couldn't bring myself to confess the truth. The result would have been me declaring my own insanity, but it wouldn't have changed the sentence given to my unfortunate victim. She perished on the scaffold like a murderer!

Overwhelmed by guilt, I shifted my focus to the profound and silent sorrow of Elizabeth. I was responsible for this too! My actions led to my father's anguish and the destruction of our once-happy home. You weep, my dear ones, but these tears won't be your last! You will cry out in sadness again and again! Frankenstein, your son, relative, and former dear friend, who would sacrifice everything for your sake, finds joy only in seeing your faces light up. He wishes only to fill your lives with blessings and serve you tirelessly. He asks you to weep, to shed countless tears. Perhaps then, if fate can be appeased and destruction paused before it claims your peace in the grave, you may find relief from your torment.

127 My inner voice spoke these words, foretelling the future, as I felt consumed by guilt, fear, and sadness. I watched those I cared for cry at the graves of William and Justine, the first tragic casualties of my forbidden experiments.

CHAPTER
NINE

128 NOTHING IS MORE painful to the human mind than the stillness and certainty that follow after intense feelings and events. It takes away hope and fear. Justine died and I was still alive. My body was full of blood, but my heart was heavy with despair and regret that couldn't be lifted. I couldn't sleep. I felt like a bad spirit because I had done terrible things that I can't even put into words. And there was more, much more, that I convinced myself I still had to do. Despite all of this, I still felt kindness and a desire to do good. I started my life with good intentions and wanted to make a difference for others. But now everything was ruined. Instead of feeling happy with what I had done in the past and looking forward to a hopeful future, I was consumed by guilt and regret. It felt like I was being dragged down into a painful place that no words could describe.

This sadness caused my health to suffer, as I had never fully recovered from the first shock I experienced. I avoided being around other people. Any sound of happiness or contentment was unbearable to me. The only thing that brought me comfort was being alone in total darkness and silence, as if I were dead.

129 My father observed my feelings and did his best to help me find

clarity and give me confidence. He asked, "Do you think, Victor," said he, "that I do not suffer also? No one could love a child more than I loved your brother. Don't feel as though you need to push back your own emotions. Feel what you need to feel."

This advice, although good, was totally inapplicable to my case. I should have been the first to comfort my friends, but instead, regret had completely taken over. Now I could only answer my father with a look of sadness, and endeavour to hide myself from his view.

130 Around this time, my family and I moved to our house in Belrive. I was really happy about this change. Living within the walls of Geneva had become frustrating because the gates closed every night at ten, and we couldn't stay out on the lake after that time. But now, I was finally free.

Sometimes, when everyone else in the family had gone to bed, I would take the boat out and spend hours on the water. With the wind in my sails, I would let it carry me. Or sometimes, I would row to the middle of the lake and let the boat go on its own while I got lost in my own sad thoughts.

There were moments when I was tempted to dive into the quiet lake, hoping it would swallow me and my troubles forever. But then I would think of Elizabeth, the brave and suffering person I loved deeply, whose life was connected to mine. I also thought about my father and my surviving brother. If I abandoned them and left them unprotected from the creature I had unleashed, it would be a cowardly act.

131 During those moments, tears streamed down my face, and I desperately wished for peace in my mind so that I could bring comfort and happiness to my loved ones. But that was impossible. Remorse crushed any hope I had. I was responsible for irreversible harm, and every day I lived in fear that the monster I had created would commit more wicked deeds. I had an inkling that it wasn't over yet, and that he would go on to do something so terrible that it would almost erase the memory of his past crimes. As long as there was something I cherished, fear would always find a way in. Words

cannot express my abhorrence for this creature. Whenever I thought of him, I clenched my teeth, my eyes burned with anger, and I wished fervently to end the life I had foolishly given him. When I considered the enormity of his crimes and his cruelty, my hatred and desire for revenge knew no bounds. If I could, I would have climbed the highest peak of the Andes just to throw him off it. I yearned to come face to face with him again, so I could unleash the full force of my abhorrence upon him and avenge the deaths of William and Justine.

132   Our house was filled with sorrow. The recent terrible events had deeply affected my father's health. Elizabeth felt sad and hopeless. She no longer found joy in her usual activities, believing that any pleasure would be disrespectful to the deceased. She thought that eternal sadness and tears were the only appropriate way to honor the innocence that had been destroyed. She was no longer the happy person she used to be when we would wander together by the lake and eagerly discuss our future. The first of the sorrows meant to detach us from earthly things had come to her, and its effects had taken away her brightest smiles.

133   "When I think about the sad death of Justine Moritz, my dear cousin," she said, "the world doesn't seem the same anymore. In the past, when I read about wrongdoing and unfairness in books or heard about it from others, I saw them as stories from long ago or make-believe. They seemed distant, something that reason under-stood better than imagination. But now, misery has arrived at our doorstep, and people seem like monsters who thirst for each other's harm. However, I know I am being unfair. Everyone believed that poor girl was guilty, and if she had really committed the crime she was accused of, she would have been the most evil person. To murder the child of her benefactor and friend, someone she had cared for since birth and loved as her own, all for a few pieces of jewelry! I could never agree to the death of any human being, but I would have believed that someone like her didn't deserve to live among society. But she was innocent. I know it, I feel it, and your

opinion supports me. Oh no, Victor, when lies can look so much like the truth, how can we ever feel certain about happiness? It feels like I'm walking on the edge of a cliff, with thousands of people pushing me towards the abyss. William and Justine were murdered, and the killer is free, maybe even respected in the world. But even if I were condemned to die for the same crimes, I would never want to switch places with such a miserable person."

134   I felt extreme agony as I listened to her words. In a way, I was the true murderer. Elizabeth could see my pain in my face, and she kindly held my hand and said, "My dearest friend, you must calm down. These events have affected me deeply, but I am not as miserable as you are. The despair and sometimes vengeful look on your face frighten me. Victor, please let go of these dark feelings. Remember the friends who care about you and want to see you happy. Have we lost the ability to make you happy? As long as we love each other in this peaceful and beautiful place, your homeland, we can have every peaceful blessing. What could disturb our peace?"

Could her words, coming from the person I cherished above all else, be enough to drive away the inner monster that haunted me? As she spoke, I moved closer to her, fearing that in that very moment, the destroyer was nearby, ready to take her away from me.

But neither the warmth of friendship nor the beauty of the world, not even the beauty of the sky, could release my soul from sadness. Even the words of love were powerless. I was surrounded by a cloud that nothing positive could break through. The wounded deer, dragging its tired legs to a hidden spot, where it could look at the arrow that had wounded it and die, was a symbol of my own situation.

135   Sometimes I could handle the deep sadness that took over me. But other times, my overwhelming emotions drove me to find relief through exercise. I suddenly left my home and headed towards the nearby Alpine valleys. I hoped that the grandeur and everlasting nature of those places would help me forget about myself and my temporary sorrows as a human. I specifically went to the Chamounix

valley, which I had visited many times when I was younger. It had been six years since my last visit, and while I was a mess, those wild and lasting scenes remained exactly the same.

136   I started my journey riding a horse. Later on, I rented a mule because they are more sure-footed and less likely to get hurt on these rough roads. The weather was nice, it was around the middle of August, almost two months after Justine died. That was a really sad time for me. But as I went deeper into the Arve ravine, I felt a bit better. The huge mountains and cliffs all around me, the sound of the river rushing through the rocks, and the waterfalls crashing down, all showed a power as strong as anything in the world. I stopped being afraid or worried about anything except for the one who made and controlled everything around me. Going higher up the valley, it became even more amazing and impressive. There were old ruined castles hanging on steep mountains covered in pine trees, the strong Arve river, and little houses popping up here and there among the trees. It was a scene of unusual beauty. But what made it even more incredible were the massive Alps. Their big, shining peaks and domes towered over everything else, like they belonged to a different world, the home of a different kind of people.

137   I crossed the Pélissier bridge and started climbing the mountain that hangs over the river's ravine. Then, I entered the Chamounix valley. This valley is amazing and grand, but not as pretty and scenic as the Servox valley I had just passed through. The tall snowy mountains were its borders, but I didn't see any more ruined castles or fertile fields. Huge glaciers came close to the road, and I heard the loud roar of the falling avalanche and saw the trail of smoke it left behind. Mount Blanc, the highest and most magnificent mountain, stood above the valley with its massive peak.

During this journey, I often felt a tingling sense of pleasure that I hadn't felt in a long time. Sometimes, a turn in the road or a new thing I saw would remind me of days gone by and bring back memories of carefree happiness from my childhood. But then, that comforting feeling would fade away—I would find myself trapped in grief once again, drowning in the misery of my thoughts. At those times, I would spur my animal forward, trying desperately to forget the world, my fears, and most of all, myself. Or in moments of complete desperation, I would get off my animal and collapse onto the grass, overwhelmed by horror and despair.

Finally, I reached the village of Chamounix. I was completely exhausted, both physically and mentally. I stood at the window for a little while, observing the faint flashes of lightning illuminating Mont Blanc and listening to the roaring sound of the Arve River rushing below. These soothing sounds acted as a lullaby, calming my intense emotions. When I laid my head on the pillow, sleep gently enveloped me. I was aware of it as it arrived, and I felt grateful for the relief it brought.

CHAPTER
TEN

139   I SPENT the next day exploring the valley. I stood next to where the Arveiron river starts, flowing from a glacier that slowly moves down from the top of the hills to block the valley. Huge mountains surrounded me, with an icy glacier hanging overhead. There were a few broken pine trees scattered around. The only sounds in this impressive place were the rushing waves of the river, the crashing of large pieces of ice falling down, and the thunderous noise of avalanches echoing through the mountains. The ice seemed invincible, yet it would occasionally break apart as if it were a toy. These amazing and stunning sights brought me the most comfort I could find. They made me feel bigger than my problems and, although they couldn't take away my sadness, they calmed and soothed me. They also helped distract my mind from the thoughts that had consumed me for the past month. When I went to sleep that night, my dreams were filled with the majestic images I had seen during the day. The pure white mountaintop, the shining peak, the pine woods, the rugged ravine, and the eagle soaring high in the sky - they all gathered around me and told me to find peace.

140   Where did they go when I woke up the next morning? All the

things that filled my soul with inspiration vanished along with sleep, and a dark sadness clouded every thought. The rain was pouring heavily, and thick fog covered the tops of the mountains, so I couldn't even see the faces of those powerful friends. But I was determined to uncover them in their misty hiding places. What did rain and storm matter to me? My mule was brought to the door, and I decided to climb up to the top of Montanvert. I remembered how the view of the enormous and constantly moving glacier had affected me the first time I saw it. It had filled me with a magnificent excitement that lifted my spirit and allowed it to rise from the ordinary world to joy and light. Seeing the awe-inspiring and majestic in nature always had the power to make me feel reverent and forget about the worries of everyday life. I made up my mind to go alone without a guide, because having someone else there would take away from the solitary magnificence of the scene.

The path up the mountain is very steep, but it has many turns that help you climb up the steep parts. The scene is extremely desolate. You can see the aftermath of the winter avalanches in many places, where trees are broken and scattered on the ground. Some trees are completely destroyed, while others are bent and leaning on the rocks or other trees. As you go higher, the path is crossed by snow-filled ravines, and stones keep rolling down from above. One of these ravines is especially dangerous because even a small sound, like speaking loudly, can bring destruction upon the person. The pine trees are not tall or lush, but they are dark and add a sense of seriousness to the scene. I looked down at the valley below, and I could see thick mists rising from the rivers that flowed through it. The mists curled around the mountains on the other side, hiding their peaks in the clouds. It was raining from the dark sky, and it made the surrounding objects feel even more sad and gloomy. Oh, why do humans take pride in having greater emotions than animals? It only makes us more vulnerable. If we only had basic needs like hunger, thirst, and desire, we could be almost free. But now, we are affected by every little thing, every word spoken or a scene we witness.

142   We take a break and a dream can ruin our sleep.

We wake up and a wandering thought spoils our day.

We experience, imagine, or think. Laugh or cry,

Hug sad sorrow, or let go of our worries...

It's all the same: whether it's happiness or sadness,

The way it disappears remains unchanged.

A person's past may never be like their future;

Nothing can last except change!

143   It was almost noon when I reached the top of the hill. I sat on a rock and looked out at the icy sea below. There was a fog covering the ice and the surrounding mountains. But then a breeze came and cleared the fog, so I started to walk down onto the glacier. The surface was bumpy, like waves on a stormy sea, with low points and deep cracks in between. The ice field was about a mile wide, and it took me almost two hours to cross it. On the other side, there was a steep rocky mountain. From where I stood, I could see Montanvert, a place about a mile away. And above it, there was Mont Blanc, a majestic mountain that looked really impressive. I found a spot in the rocks and just stared at this amazing scene. The ice river wound its way through the mountains, with their tall peaks shining in the sunlight above the clouds. My heart, which had been sad before, now felt a little happy. I couldn't help but say, "If there are wandering spirits out there, please let me have this small happiness, or take me with you, away from the troubles of life."

144   As I spoke, I suddenly saw a man in the distance, coming towards me faster than any human could. He leaped over the cracks in the ice, where I had been walking carefully. As he got closer, I realized that he was taller than an ordinary person. I was afraid and felt dizzy, but the cold wind from the mountains brought me back to my senses. I saw, with horror, that the approaching figure was the monster I had created. I shook with anger and fear, deciding to confront him and fight him to the death. He came closer, his face showing both

anguish and hatred, and his unnatural ugliness made him almost too terrible to look at. But I was too consumed by rage and hatred to notice. At first, I couldn't speak because of my intense emotions, but then I found my voice and unleashed a torrent of furious hatred and contempt upon him.

"You monster!" I shouted. "How dare you come near me? Aren't you afraid of the fierce vengeance that will befall you? Leave, you disgusting creature! No, stay! I want to crush you into dust! Oh, if only I could bring back the innocent lives you have cruelly taken away!"

145   "I expected this," said the monster. "All men hate the wretched, I know I am hated! Yet you, my creator, hate me, too! You want to kill me. Do your duty towards me, and I will do mine towards you and the rest of mankind. If you will comply with my conditions, I will leave them and you at peace. However, if you refuse, I will glut the maw of death, until it be satiated with the blood of your remaining friends."

"Monster! Wretched devil! You hate me for your creation and now I will extinguish your life!"

My rage was without bounds. I sprang on him, impelled by all the feelings which can arm one being against the existence of another.

He easily eluded me, and said—

146   "Please, calm down! I beg you to listen to me before you unleash your anger on me. Haven't I suffered enough? Why do you want to make me even more miserable? Life, even if it's filled with pain, is precious to me, and I will protect it. Remember, you made me more powerful than you. I'm taller and more flexible. But I won't be tempted to fight against you. I am your creation, and I will be gentle and obedient to my natural creator and ruler if you do your part too. Oh, Frankenstein, don't treat me unfairly while being kind to everyone else. Remember, I am your creation. I should be like your Adam, but instead, I feel like a fallen angel, cast out of happiness for no reason. Everywhere I look, I see joy that I can never experience. I

used to be kind and good, but misery turned me into a monster. Make me happy, and I will become virtuous once again."

"Go away! I won't listen to you. We can never have a relationship. We are enemies. Leave, or let's test our strength in a fight where one of us must be defeated."

147   "How can I persuade you? Can't my pleas make you look kindly upon your creation, who begs for your goodness and compassion? Believe me, Frankenstein, I used to be kind-hearted; my soul was filled with love and humanity. But now, am I not alone, terribly alone? You, my creator, despise me. What hope can I have from other people, who owe me nothing? They reject and hate me. The empty mountains and cold icy caves are my only refuge. I have wandered here for many days, finding solace only in these icy caves that even humans don't want. I welcome these harsh skies, for they treat me better than your fellow human beings. If the world knew about me, they would do what you do - arm themselves to destroy me. Shouldn't I hate those who despise me then? I won't make peace with my enemies. I am miserable, and they should experience my misery too. But you have the power to repay me and save them from the evil that you can make so great, that not only you and your family, but thousands of others will be destroyed by it. Please, be compassionate and don't reject me. Listen to my story. Once you've heard it, you can abandon me or feel sorry for me as you think I deserve. But please listen to me. Even criminals, by human laws, are allowed to defend themselves before they are condemned. Listen to me, Frankenstein. You accuse me of murder, yet you would, without a second thought, destroy your own creation. Oh, what a testament to the eternal justice of humanity! But I don't ask you to spare me. Listen to me, and then, if you can, if you want to, destroy what you have made."

148   "Why are you reminding me," I replied, "of things that fill me with fear and regret, knowing that I am the miserable cause and creator of them? Cursed be the day, hated devil, when you first came

into existence! Go away! Spare me from the sight of your detestable form."

"Then I will spare you, my creator," he said sadly, covering my eyes with his hands, which I forcefully pushed away. "I will take away a sight that you despise. But you can still listen to me and show me compassion. I beg this of you based on the goodness I once possessed. Hear my story. It's up to you to determine if I leave humanity forever and live a peaceful life, or if I become a punishment to your fellow humans and the cause of your own inevitable destruction."

As he said that, he went ahead on the ice and I followed. My heart was full and I didn't answer him, but as we walked, I considered the different things he said and decided to at least hear his story. I was curious and felt sorry for him, which made me stick to my decision. I used to think he was the one who killed my brother, so I really wanted to confirm or deny this belief. It was also the first time I realized that as his creator, I had a duty to make him happy before I complained about his bad actions. These reasons made me agree to his request. So, we walked across the ice and climbed up the other side. It was cold and it started raining again. We went into the hut, the creature looking pleased, while I felt sad and downhearted. But I agreed to listen and sat down by the fire he had lit. That's when he began his story.

CHAPTER

ELEVEN

 "It's really hard for me to remember the very beginning of my existence. Everything from that time is jumbled and unclear in my mind. I experienced a strange mix of sensations – seeing, feeling, hearing, and smelling all at once. It took me a long time to figure out how to tell them apart. Gradually, I recall a brighter light overwhelming my senses, so I had to close my eyes. Darkness surrounded me and made me uneasy, but as soon as I opened my eyes, the light flooded back in. I walked, and maybe even went downhill, but things started to feel different. Before, I was surrounded by dark and solid objects that I couldn't see through or touch. But now, I could freely move around without any obstacles blocking my way. The light kept getting stronger and more overwhelming, and the heat made me tired as I walked. I looked for a place where I could find some shade. That's when I found a forest near Ingolstadt. I rested next to a stream, recovering from my exhaustion. But soon, hunger and thirst started to bother me. That woke me up from my almost sleeping state, and I ate some berries hanging from the trees or lying on the ground. I quenched my thirst from the stream and then lay down, falling asleep."

151   I woke up and it was dark. I felt cold and a little scared because I was all alone. Before I left your room, I had covered myself with some clothes because I felt cold. But they didn't keep me warm enough from the night's dew. I was a poor, helpless, and miserable person. I didn't know or understand anything, but I felt pain all over, so I sat down and cried.

Then, a soft light started to brighten the sky and it made me feel happy. I stood up and saw a glowing figure emerging from the trees. I looked at it with amazement. It moved slowly but lit up my way, so I went out to find berries again. I was still cold, but I found a big cloak under one of the trees. I covered myself with it and sat on the ground. My thoughts were jumbled and confused. I felt light, hungry, thirsty, and surrounded by darkness. I heard many different sounds and smelled different scents all around me. The only thing I could clearly see was the bright moon, and I focused my gaze on it with delight.

152   Several days and nights passed, and the moon had gotten smaller when I began to understand my feelings. I could clearly see the stream that gave me water and the trees that provided shade with their leaves. I felt happy when I realized that the pleasant sound I often heard came from the little winged animals that flew around me.

The moon had disappeared from the night sky and appeared again, but it was smaller. I was still in the forest. By this time, I could understand my feelings better, and my mind was getting new ideas every day. My eyes adjusted to the light and I could see objects clearly in their proper shapes. I could tell the difference between insects and plants, and gradually learned to distinguish one plant from another. I discovered that sparrows made harsh sounds, while blackbirds and thrushes made sweet and inviting songs.

153   One day, on a cold day, I found an abandoned fire left by some beggars. I was overjoyed by the warmth it gave me. In my excitement, I touched the live embers with my hand but quickly pulled it away because it hurt. It was strange to me how the same thing could

have such different effects. I looked at the fire closely and was happy to see that it was made of wood. I tried to gather some branches, but they were wet and wouldn't burn. This made me sad, so I sat and watched the fire. As the wet branches got closer to the heat, they dried out and caught fire on their own. I thought about this and touched different branches to figure out why. Then, I started collecting a lot of wood so I could dry it and have plenty of fire. When night came and I got sleepy, I was really scared that my fire would go out. I covered it carefully with dry wood and leaves and put wet branches on top. Then, I spread out my cloak on the ground and fell into a deep sleep.

154   When I woke up in the morning, my first priority was to check on the fire. I uncovered it, and a gentle breeze quickly made it become a flame. I noticed this and thought of a way to keep the embers alive when they were almost dying out. I made a fan out of branches, which helped to revive the fire. When night came again, I was happy to see that the fire not only provided heat but also gave off light. I realized that this discovery was helpful for cooking my food. I found some leftovers that the travelers had left behind, and they were roasted. They tasted much better than the berries I usually ate from the trees. So, I tried to cook my food the same way by placing it on the live embers. I learned that this made the berries go bad, but it improved the taste of nuts and roots.

155   "Food became hard to find, and I often spent the whole day searching, but couldn't find many acorns to ease my hunger. When I realized this, I decided to leave the place I had been staying in and look for somewhere else where it would be easier to find the few things I needed. I was really sad to lose the fire that I had accidentally started and didn't know how to make another one. I thought about this problem for a long time, but couldn't figure out a solution. I spent three days exploring and finally found open fields. There had been a big snowfall the night before, and everything was covered in white. It looked sad and made me feel cold."

156   It was early in the morning, around seven o'clock, and I really

needed to find some food and a place to stay. Finally, I spotted a small hut up on a hill. It was probably made for a shepherd to use. This was something new for me, so I was very curious and went to take a closer look at it. Luckily, the door was open, so I went inside. There was an old man sitting there by a fire, cooking his breakfast. When he heard me, he screamed and quickly ran away across the fields, even though he seemed weak. I was a bit surprised by his strange appearance and sudden escape, but I was more fascinated by the hut itself. It was a shelter where the snow and rain couldn't get in, and the ground was dry. To me, it felt like a wonderful place, just like how hell would appear to the demons in the story of Pandæmonium once they got out of their suffering in the lake of fire. I eagerly ate what was left of the shepherd's breakfast - some bread, cheese, milk, and wine - though I didn't really like the taste of the wine. After that, I was so tired that I lay down in some straw and fell asleep.

157   I woke up at noon and was enticed by the warm sun shining on the snowy ground. I decided it was time to continue my journey. I gathered the leftover food from the peasant's breakfast in a bag I discovered and set off across the fields for several hours. By sunset, I reached a village, and it was like a miracle to me! The simple huts, cozy cottages, and grand houses took turns capturing my admiration. The sight of vegetables in the gardens and milk and cheese displayed at some cottage windows made my stomach growl with hunger. Curious, I stepped into one of the nicer cottages, but as soon as I entered, the children screamed and one of the women fainted. The whole village was alarmed, and some people ran away while others attacked me. I was hit by stones and various objects until I escaped to the open countryside, battered and bruised. Fearfully, I found refuge in a small, rundown hovel that appeared even worse compared to the magnificent palaces I had seen in the village. However, this hovel was connected to a neat and pleasant-looking cottage. After my recent terrifying experience, I didn't dare enter the cottage. The hovel I was in was made of wood and so low that it was difficult for me to sit upright. The floor was made of earth, but it was

dry. Despite the wind coming in through many cracks, it provided a pleasant shelter from the snow and rain.

So I found a miserable shelter to escape the bad weather and cruel people. In the morning, I left my hideout to take a look at the nearby cottage. It was located at the back of the cottage, with a pigsty. I had enough light coming through it, which was good enough for me.

After arranging my new home and spreading clean straw on the floor, I went to rest. I spotted a man in the distance and remembered how I was treated the previous night, so I didn't want to risk being caught. But before that, I made sure I had enough food for the day. I took a loaf of coarse bread and a cup to drink water from the nearby stream more easily. The floor was slightly raised to keep it dry, and being close to the cottage's chimney made it somewhat warm.

With my basic necessities obtained, I made up my mind to stay in this hovel until something happened that might change my decision. Compared to the desolate forest where I used to live, with its branches dripping rain and damp earth, this place was a paradise. I enjoyed my breakfast and was getting ready to remove a plank to get some water when I heard footsteps. Peeking through a small hole, I saw a young girl carrying a pail on her head passing by my hovel. She had a kind and gentle manner, unlike the people I later found living in cottages and working on farms. She was dressed modestly, wearing a plain blue skirt and a simple jacket. Her fair hair was braided but not styled, and she looked patient yet sad. She disappeared from my view, but after about fifteen minutes, she returned with the pail, which was now partially filled with milk. As she walked, struggling with the heavy load, a young man approached her, looking even more hopeless. He spoke a few words with a melancholic expression, then took the pail from her and carried it to the cottage himself. She followed behind, and they vanished inside. After a while, I saw the young man again, holding some tools as he crossed the field behind the cottage. The girl was also busy, going back and forth between the house and the yard.

160 I inspected my dwelling and noticed that one of the windows used to be a part of the cottage, but it had been covered up with wood. In one of the wooden panels, there was a tiny gap that allowed a glimpse inside. Through this gap, I could see a small room that was clean but hardly had any furniture. Sitting in the corner, by a small fire, was an elderly man who seemed very sad, resting his head on his hands. The young girl was busy arranging the cottage, but then she took something out of a drawer and sat down next to the old man. As he picked up an instrument, he started playing the most beautiful music, even sweeter than the songs of birds. It was a captivating scene, especially for me, who had never seen anything so lovely before. The old man's silver hair and kind face earned my respect, and the girl's gentle behavior captured my affection. He played a hauntingly sad melody that made the girl start to cry. The old man didn't say anything until she sobbed out loud. Then he made a few sounds, and the girl stopped working, knelt down in front of him. He lifted her up and smiled at her with such kindness and love that I felt a mix of intense emotions. It was a strange and powerful feeling, unlike anything I had experienced from being hungry, cold, warm, or fed. Overwhelmed, I stepped away from the window, unable to handle these strong feelings.

161 Soon after this, the young man came back carrying a bundle of wood on his shoulders. The girl greeted him at the door and helped him to unload the wood. They brought some of the wood into the cottage and added it to the fire. Then, they both went to a cozy corner of the cottage, where the young man showed her a big loaf of bread and a piece of cheese. They carried on with different tasks.

162 "The old man had been lost in thought, but when his companions arrived, he became more cheerful, and they sat down to eat. They finished their meal quickly. The young woman started tidying up the cottage, while the old man took a short walk in the sun, leaning on the young man's arm. These two individuals were very different, yet they complemented each other beautifully. The old man had silver hair and a kind, loving face. The young man had a

slim and graceful figure, and his features were perfectly balanced. But his eyes and body language showed deep sadness and hopelessness. The old man went back inside the cottage, and the young man, with different tools than before, headed across the fields."

163 Night came quickly, and I was astonished to see that the people in the cottage had a way to keep the light going by using candles. I was excited to discover that when the sun went down, I could still watch my neighbors. I observed them doing something that I didn't recognize. I later learned that the young man was reading aloud, but at that time, I didn't know anything about words or letters.

After spending a short time doing these things, the family put out their lights and went to bed, or so I guessed.

CHAPTER

TWELVE

 I LAY ON MY STRAW, but I couldn't sleep. I thought about what happened during the day. What stood out to me the most was how kind and polite these people were. I wanted to join them, but I was too afraid. I remembered how the villagers treated me badly the night before, so I decided to stay quietly in my little shack for now. I would watch them and try to understand why they did what they did.

The next morning, the cottagers woke up before the sun. The young woman tidied up the cottage and made breakfast, while the young man left after eating.

The day went on just like the day before. The young man was always busy outside, and the girl had different hard tasks to do inside. The old man, who I realized was blind, spent his free time playing his instrument or thinking. The younger cottagers treated him with so much love and respect. They took care of him with kindness and he smiled at them to show his gratitude.

 They were not completely happy. Sometimes, the young man and his friend would separate and seem to cry. I didn't understand why they were so sad, but it deeply affected me. If these wonderful beings were unhappy, it made sense that I, as an imperfect and lonely creature, would feel miserable too. But why were these kind creatures unhappy? They had a lovely house (at least in my eyes) and everything they could want. They had a warm fire when they were cold, and delicious food when they were hungry. They were dressed in nice clothes, and, most importantly, they had each other. They showed affection and kindness every day. So, what was the reason behind their tears? Did they truly feel pain? At first, I couldn't figure out the answers to these questions. But with careful observation and time, I started to understand some of the things that confused me at first.

It took a while before I discovered one of the reasons why this kind family felt so uneasy: it was because of poverty. They suffered from it a lot. They survived only on the vegetables they grew in their garden and the little amount of milk their cow provided, especially during the winter when it was hard to find enough food for the cow. I believe they often went hungry, especially the younger members of the family. Many times, they would give food to the old man while keeping none for themselves.

The kindness of the cottagers touched my heart. At night, I used to take some of their food for myself, but when I realized it caused them pain, I stopped. Instead, I satisfied my hunger with berries, nuts, and roots that I found in a nearby forest.

I also found another way to help them. The young man would gather wood all day for their fire. At night, I would take his tools and bring back enough wood to last them for several days.

I remember the first time I did this, the young woman was surprised when she opened the door in the morning and saw a big pile of wood. She said something loudly, and the young man joined her, also looking surprised. I was happy to see that he didn't go to the forest that day. Instead, he spent the day fixing the cottage and tending to the garden.

Gradually, I made an important discovery. These people had a way of sharing their experiences and feelings using spoken words. I noticed that the words they used could make others feel happy or sad, and even make them smile or look sad. It was like a special power, and I really wanted to learn it. But no matter how hard I tried, I couldn't figure it out. They spoke quickly, and the words they used didn't seem to have any connection to things I could see. I couldn't find a clue to unlock the mystery. However, after spending many months in my little house, I finally learned the names they used for familiar things. I learned words like fire, milk, bread, and wood. I also learned their names. The young man and his friend had multiple names, but the old man was called father, the girl was called sister or Agatha, and the young man was called brother or son. I can't even begin to describe how happy I was when I understood what these words meant and could say them myself. I also recognized some other words, even though I didn't know exactly what they meant yet. Words like good, dearest, and unhappy.

168   I spent the winter like this. The people living in the cottage were kind and nice, and I really liked them. When they were sad, it made me feel sad too. And when they were happy, I shared in their happiness. I didn't see many other people besides them, but if anyone else did come to the cottage, I thought they were rude and not as good as my friends. I could tell that the old man tried to make his children, whom he sometimes called, feel better when they were sad. He would speak in a happy voice and had a kind expression that made me happy too. Agatha listened to him with respect and sometimes had tears in her eyes that she tried to hide. But I noticed that after listening to her father, she seemed to be happier. Felix, on the other hand, was always the saddest of the group. Even though I didn't have a lot of experience, I could see that he had gone through tough times. But even though he looked sad, his voice sounded cheerful when he talked to the old man, especially.

169   I saw many examples that showed the kind nature of these friendly people. Even though they were poor and lacking basic necessities, Felix would bring the first little white flower that peeked out from under the snow to his sister, and it made her happy. Before

she woke up in the morning, he would clear a path for her to the milk-house by removing the snow. He would also get water from the well and bring firewood from the out-house. During the day, he sometimes worked for a nearby farmer and didn't come back until dinner time, but he never brought wood with him. Other times, he worked in the garden. Since there wasn't much to do in the cold season, he would read to the old man and Agatha.

170   This reading confused me a lot at first, but then I realized that the man made similar sounds when he read as when he talked. So, I figured that he understood the signs on the paper as words. I really wanted to understand them too, but how could I when I didn't understand the sounds they represented? I had a thought. If I knew their language, maybe they would look past my appearance, which I could always see in contrast to their beauty.

I admired the cottagers' perfect looks – how graceful and beautiful they were with their smooth skin. But when I saw my reflection in a clear pool. I realized I was an absolute monster. Little did I know the awful consequences of looking like this.

171   As the sun got hotter and the days got longer, Felix had more work to do, and the signs of an upcoming shortage of food disappeared. Their food, I later learned, was rough but good for them, and they were able to get enough of it. New plants started growing in the garden.

The old man leaned on his son and they went for a walk every day at noon, unless it was raining, which is what they called it when water poured down from the sky. This happened often, but a strong wind quickly dried the ground, and the season became much more enjoyable than before.

172   My daily routine in my small shelter was the same every day. In the morning, I would watch what the cottagers were doing, and when they were busy with their tasks, I would sleep. The rest of the day, I would observe my friends. At night, if there was a moon or the stars were shining, I would go to the woods and gather my own food and firewood for the cottage. When I came back, I would clear the

snow from their path and do the same helpful things that I had seen Felix do. Later on, I found out that they were amazed at these chores being done by someone they couldn't see. Sometimes, I heard them say things like "good spirit" and "wonderful" on these occasions, but I didn't understand the meaning of those words at the time.

173   I began to think more and became curious about the feelings and reasons behind the sadness of Felix and Agatha, these kind people. I foolishly believed that I could make them happy again. When I slept or wasn't around, I would dream of the wise, blind father, the gentle Agatha, and the excellent Felix. If I could only meet them, I thought they would be disgusted at first, until I won them over with my kind behavior and friendly words, eventually earning their love.

These thoughts made me excited and motivated me to work even harder on learning their language. I knew it had to be a way to win their love and respect.

174   The warm spring rains and sunshine made the earth look different. People who used to hide in caves came out and started doing different kinds of farming. The birds started singing with more joy, and the tree leaves started growing. The earth was so happy and perfect, even though not long ago it was cold, wet, and unhealthy. Seeing the beautiful nature made me feel happy and forget about the past. Everything felt calm now, and I felt hopeful and excited about the future.

THIRTEEN

175 I NOW WANT to talk about the most emotional part of my story. I will tell you about events that made me feel things that changed me from who I was before.

As spring came, the weather got better and the skies were clear. I was surprised to see that the places that were empty and dark before were now filled with beautiful flowers and greenness.

On one of those days, when the people in the cottages took a break from their work, the old man played his guitar and the children listened to him. But I noticed that Felix, the son, had a very sad look on his face. He sighed a lot, and at one point his father stopped playing and seemed to ask him why he was sad. Felix answered in a cheerful voice, and the old man started playing his music again, when someone knocked on the door.

176 "It was a lady on horseback, accompanied by a countryman as a guide. The lady was dressed in a dark suit, and covered with a thick black veil. Agatha asked a question to which the stranger only replied by pronouncing, in a sweet accent, the name of Felix. Her voice was musical, but unlike that of either of my friends. On hearing

this word, Felix came up quickly. The woman revealed her beautiful face and hair. She was breathtaking.

177   Felix was overjoyed when he saw her. All of his sadness disappeared, and his face instantly lit up with extreme happiness, which I didn't think was possible. His eyes sparkled, and his cheeks turned red with joy. In that moment, I thought he looked as beautiful as the lady. She seemed to have different emotions. She wiped a few tears from her eyes and reached out her hand to Felix, who kissed it with great excitement. He called her something like "his sweet Arabian," but she didn't seem to understand. She just smiled. He helped her get off the horse and told her guide to leave. Then, he led her into the cottage. He had a conversation with his father, and the young lady knelt in front of the old man. She wanted to kiss his hand, but he lifted her up and hugged her affectionately.

178   I quickly noticed that even though the stranger spoke in a way that sounded like real words. They used gestures that I couldn't figure out, but I could see that her presence brought happiness to the cottage. Felix was especially happy and warmly welcomed the stranger. Agatha, always kind-hearted, kissed the hands of the lovely stranger. She pointed to her brother and made signs that seemed to mean he had been sad until she arrived. A few hours went by like this, with their faces showing joy, though I didn't understand why. Then I noticed that the stranger was repeating a sound after them over and over again, trying to learn their language. That gave me the idea to use the same lessons to learn too. The stranger learned about twenty words in the first lesson. I already knew most of them, but I learned some new ones too.

179   As night arrived, Agatha and the Arabian went to bed early. When they said goodbye, Felix kissed the stranger's hand and said, "Good night, sweet Safie." He talked of her often after that time.

The next morning, Felix went to work, and after Agatha finished her usual tasks, the Arabian sat by the old man's feet. She picked up his guitar and played some incredibly beautiful songs that made me feel both sad and happy. The old man seemed captivated and said something that Agatha tried to explain to Safie. He seemed to want to express how much joy her music brought him.

180   The days continued peacefully, and my friends' expressions of sadness were replaced by joy. Safie and I made great progress in learning the language, and within two months, I could understand most of what my protectors said.

During this time, the ground turned black and was covered in plants, while the green banks displayed countless lovely flowers that smelled sweet and looked beautiful. I enjoyed nighttime walks, but I was afraid to venture out during the day, remembering the mistreatment I had experienced in the first village I encountered.

I dedicated my days to learning the language with intense focus. I also learned how to read and write, just as the stranger had been taught. This opened up a fascinating world of knowledge and brought me great joy.

181   The book that Felix used to teach Safie was called Volney's "Ruins of Empires." I wouldn't have understood this book if Felix hadn't explained it in great detail while reading. He chose this book because it was written in a style similar to that of Eastern authors. By reading this book, I gained a basic understanding of history and learned about the different empires that exist in the world today. It gave me a glimpse into the customs, governments, and religions of various nations. I learned about the laid-back people of Asia, the impressive intelligence and creativity of the Greeks, and the wars and remarkable virtues of the early Romans. I also learned about the gradual decline of the powerful Roman Empire, as well as the concepts of chivalry, Christianity, and kings. I discovered the story of how the Americas were found, and I felt sad along with Safie for the unfortunate fate of the original inhabitants.

182   "These wonderful narrations inspired me. To be a great and virtuous man appeared the highest honour and to be cruel and dumb, the worst thing a man could be. For a long time I could not understand how one man could go and murder his fellow, or even why there were laws and governments. When I heard details of vice

and bloodshed, my wonder ceased, and I turned away with disgust and loathing.

"Every conversation of the cottagers now opened new wonders to me. While I listened to the instructions which Felix bestowed upon the Arabian, the strange system of human society was explained to me. I learned so much.

The words made me think about myself. I learned that people value two things the most: being born into a rich and respected family. If someone had only one of these things, they would still be respected. But if they had neither, they were seen as worthless and treated like a slave, forced to work for the wealthy few. And what about me? I didn't have any money, friends, or any kind of belongings. On top of that, I had a horribly ugly and repulsive appearance. I wasn't even the same kind of being as humans. I was faster and could survive on less food. I could handle extreme temperatures better. And I was much taller than them. When I looked around, I didn't see anyone like me. Did that mean I was a monster? Did everyone run away and reject me?

I can't even describe how much pain these thoughts caused me. I tried to forget about them, but the more I knew, the sadder I became. Oh, I wish I had stayed in my forest forever, unaware and untouched by anything beyond feeling hungry, thirsty, and hot.

"Knowledge is a strange thing! Once it gets into your mind, it sticks around like a little plant on a rock. Sometimes, I wanted to get rid of all thoughts and feelings. But I found out that the only way to stop feeling the pain was death, which scared me, even though I didn't really understand it. I admired good behavior and kind feelings. I loved how the people in the cottages were so polite and nice. But I couldn't interact with them openly. I could only secretly watch them and learn from them without them knowing. It only made me want to be a part of their world even more. The kind words from Agatha and the happy smiles from the Arabian person were not meant for me. The wise advice from the old man and the fun conversations from Felix, who I loved, were not meant for me. I was a miserable, unhappy person!

I also learned other important lessons. I heard about the differences between boys and girls. I learned about how babies are born and grow up. I saw how fathers loved the smiles of their babies and enjoyed playing with their older children. I saw how mothers dedicated their lives to taking care of their kids. I learned how young people's minds grow and gain knowledge. I learned about siblings and all the different ways people are connected to each other as family."

But where were my friends and family? No father had watched over me when I was a baby, and no mother had shown me love with smiles and hugs. Or maybe they did, but it's all a blur, a blank space in my memory where I can't remember anything. As far back as I can remember, I looked the same in height and shape. I had never seen anyone who looked like me or claimed to know me. Who was I? The question kept coming back, and the only response was to groan in frustration.

I will explain soon where these feelings were leading me, but let me go back to talking about the people in the cottages. Their story made me feel so many different things - anger, happiness, and amazement. But in the end, it all turned into even more love and admiration for my protectors (that's what I liked to call them, even though it was a naive way to deceive myself).

FOURTEEN

186   IT TOOK some time before I came to know the story of my friends. It was a tale that deeply impressed me.

The old man, whose name was De Lacey, came from a respectable family in France. He had lived there for many years, enjoying a life of prosperity and earning the respect of those around him. His son served their country, while Agatha mingled with noble-women of high status. Just a few months before I arrived, they resided in a grand and lavish city called Paris. They were surrounded by friends and had everything they could desire – a combination of virtue, intellect, refinement, and a comfortable fortune.

The downfall of the De Lacey family came at the hands of Safie's father. He was a merchant from Turkey who had been living in Paris for many years. For reasons unknown to me, he became a target of the government. On the very day Safie arrived from Constantinople to join him, he was arrested and thrown into prison. He was then put on trial and sentenced to death. The unfairness of his punishment was glaringly evident, and the people of Paris were outraged. It was believed that his religion and wealth, rather than the supposed crime, led to what happened to him.

187   Felix happened to be at the trial by accident. He was horrified and furious when he heard the court's decision. In that moment, he made a solemn promise to rescue the prisoner and started searching for a way to do it. After several unsuccessful attempts to enter the prison, he finally discovered a heavily barred window in an unguarded area of the building. This window provided light to the dungeon where the unfortunate prisoner, a Muslim man named Mahometan, was being held in chains. Mahometan was waiting in despair for the cruel punishment to be executed. At night, Felix visited the window and revealed his plan to help the prisoner. Mahometan was astonished and grateful, trying to motivate Felix by offering him rewards and wealth. But Felix refused these offers with disdain. However, when he saw the beautiful Safie, who was permitted to visit her father, and saw her expressing deep gratitude through her gestures, Felix couldn't help but feel that the captive possessed a treasure that would make all his efforts and risks worthwhile.

The Turk, Mahometan, quickly noticed the effect his daughter had on Felix's heart. He tried to gain Felix's complete loyalty by promising him Safie's hand in marriage once they both reached a safe place. However, Felix was too honorable to accept this offer directly. Still, he couldn't help but anticipate the possibility of this happening, as it would bring him great joy and fulfillment.

188   During the next few days, while they were getting ready for the merchant to escape, Felix felt even more determined after receiving some letters from the girl. Even though she couldn't speak his language, she found a way to communicate. In those letters, she thanked Felix for helping her father and expressed sadness about her own situation.

I have copies of these letters because I found writing materials when I was living in the hovel. Felix and Agatha would often read them. Before I leave, I'll give you the letters as proof of my story. But for now, since the sun is going down, I only have time to tell you the main points.

189   Safie explained that her mother was responsible for her independence of spirit, forbidden to the female followers of Mahomet. This lady died but her lessons were impressed on the mind of Safie, who sickened at the idea of again returning to Asia. This would only lead her to isolation and a life she didn't want. The prospect of marrying a Christian, and remaining in a country where women were allowed to take a rank in society, was enchanting to her.

"The day for the execution of the Turk was fixed, but, on the night previous to it, he quitted his prison, and before morning was distant many leagues from Paris. Felix had procured passports in the name of his father, sister, and himself. He had previously communicated his plan to the former, who helped by quitting his house, under the pretence of a journey, and concealed himself, with his daughter, in an obscure part of Paris.

190   Felix guided the escaped group across France, where the merchant intended to find the right opportunity to enter the Turkish territories.

Safie made up her mind to stay with her father until he left. Felix stayed with them, eagerly waiting for that moment. In the meantime, he enjoyed the company of Safie. Safie delighted Felix by singing beautiful songs from her homeland.

The Turk allowed Safie and Felix's closeness to grow and even encouraged their young love, hiding his true intentions in his heart. He secretly despised the idea of his daughter marrying a Christian, but he feared Felix's anger if he showed any sign of disapproval. The Turk knew that he still depended on Felix to keep their secret, as he could expose them to the Italian authorities if he wanted to. The Turk came up with multiple plans to keep up the deception until it became unnecessary. He would then secretly bring his daughter with him when he left. The news that arrived from Paris aided his schemes.

191   The French government was very angry when their prisoner escaped, and they tried hard to find and punish the person who helped him. Felix's plan was quickly uncovered, and De Lacey and

Agatha were put into prison. When Felix heard the news, it woke him up from his happy thoughts. His old and blind father, and his kind sister, were trapped in a dirty cell while he enjoyed freedom outside and the company of his beloved. This idea tortured him. He quickly made a deal with the Turks that if they found a good chance to escape before Felix could go back to Italy, Safie would stay at a convent in Leghorn. Then, leaving his dear Arabian companion behind, he hurried to Paris and turned himself in to the law, hoping to save De Lacey and Agatha.

But he failed. They were kept locked up for five months until the trial happened, and they were stripped of their wealth and forced to leave their homeland forever.

They found a miserable place to stay in a cottage in Germany, where I found them. Felix soon learned that the deceitful Turk, who had brought so much suffering to him and his family, had become a traitor to kindness and honor. The Turk left Italy with his daughter and sent Felix a small amount of money, as if to mock him, saying it could help him find a way to support himself in the future.

192 Such were the things that weighed heavily on Felix's heart and made him the unhappiest person in his family when I first met him. He could have handled being poor, and if he had to suffer because of his goodness, he would have been proud of it. But the Turk's ungratefulness and losing his beloved Safie were much worse and couldn't be fixed. Then, when the Arabian arrived, Felix felt alive again.

When the news reached Leghorn that Felix had lost all his money and his social status, the merchant told his daughter to forget about her lover and start getting ready to go back to their home country. Safie didn't like this and tried to talk to her father about it, but he left and was very angry.

A few days later, the Turk went into his daughter's room and quickly told her that he had reason to believe that people in Leghorn knew where they were. He thought that the French government would soon capture him. So, he hired a ship to take him to Constantinople, and he would set sail in a few hours. He planned to leave his daughter with a trusted servant and she would come later with most of his money, which hadn't arrived in Leghorn yet.

193 When Safie was alone, she thought about what she should do in this difficult situation. She really didn't want to live in Turkey because it went against her religion and her feelings. She found some papers that belonged to her dad, and they mentioned that her lover was exiled and told her where he was living now. She thought about it for a while, but finally made up her mind. She took some of her jewelry and some money, and with a servant from Leghorn who could speak Turkish, she left Italy and went to Germany.

She made it safely to a town not far from De Lacey's cottage, but her servant got very sick. Safie took care of her with all her heart, but sadly, the servant died. Now Safie was all alone and didn't know the language of the country or anything about how things worked there. But luckily, she ended up in good hands. The Italian had mentioned the name of the place they were going to, and after the servant died, the woman who owned the house where they had stayed made sure that Safie arrived safely at her lover's cottage.

CHAPTER

FIFTEEN

194   "Such was the history of my beloved cottagers. It impressed me deeply. I thought of them as such kind people.

"However, I was also in a period of learning. One important event happened in the beginning of the month of August of the same year.

"One night, during my visit to the neighbouring wood, where I collected my own food, and brought home firing for my protectors, I found on the ground a bundle of stories. It was so strange to find, but I was also really excited to go back to my hovel and read them. I had acquired 'Paradise Lost,' a volume of 'Plutarch's Lives,' and the 'Sorrows of Werter.' I was delighted-- an exercise for my mind!

195   I can't fully explain what these books did to me. They made me feel so many new things and imagine so many new images. Sometimes, they made me really happy. But most of the time, they made me really sad. In 'The Sorrows of Werter,' besides the interesting and sad story, it talked about a lot of different ideas that were confusing to me before. It made me think and wonder about things all the time. The book described kind and loving people who also had big dreams. It reminded me of the people who took care of me and the things I

86

wanted in life. But I thought Werter was even more amazing than any real person I had seen. He didn't pretend to be anyone else, and that made a big impression on me. The parts about death and suicide were really surprising. I didn't totally understand them, but I felt really sad for the hero, even if I didn't know why.

196   As I read, I couldn't help but apply the words to my own feelings and situation. I saw similarities between myself and the characters in the book, but also noticed some differences. I understood and felt for them, but I was still growing and figuring things out. I didn't depend on anyone, and no one depended on me. I had the freedom to go wherever I wanted, and no one would feel sad if I disappeared. People thought I looked awful and enormous. What did that mean? Who was I? What was I? Where did I come from? Where was I going? These questions kept coming up, but I couldn't find the answers.

197   I owned a book called "Plutarch's Lives" that told the stories of the first leaders of ancient republics. Reading this book was very different from reading "Sorrows of Werter." While Werter made me feel sad and gloomy, Plutarch's book inspired me with good thoughts. It lifted me up from my own sad thoughts. I read about people involved in government and wars. It made me passionate about doing good and detest acting badly. I started to admire peaceful lawmakers like Numa, Solon, and Lycurgus, more than aggressive leaders like Romulus and Theseus. With the way my guardians lived their lives, these ideas became very important to me. If my first encounter with people had been through a young soldier who wanted glory and to harm others, maybe I would have felt differently.

198   But 'Paradise Lost' made me feel something completely different and much stronger. I read it as if it were a true story, just like the other books I had read before. It stirred up all sorts of amazing and awe-inspiring feelings. I couldn't help but be amazed at the image of a powerful God fighting against his own creations. Sometimes, I found similarities between the situations in the book and my own life.

Like Adam, it seemed like I had no connection to anyone else in the world. But that's where the similarities ended. Adam was created perfectly by God, he was happy and had everything he needed. He could even talk to and learn from superior beings. But I was miserable, helpless, and all alone. Often, I saw myself more like Satan, feeling bitter envy when I looked at how happy my protectors were.

199   Another thing happened that made my feelings even stronger. Soon after I arrived in the small shack, I found some papers in the pocket of the dress I took from your lab. At first, I didn't pay much attention to them. But when I learned how to read the words written on them, I started studying them carefully. Those papers were your journal from the four months before I was created. You wrote down every step you took while working on your project. You also wrote about things happening in your home. You probably remember these papers. Here they are. They tell everything about my miserable beginning. They describe in great detail all the awful things that happened to lead to my existence. They even include a very detailed description of my disgusting appearance. Reading it made me feel sick. "What a terrible day it was when I came to life!" I cried out in agony. "You, the one who made me, why did you create such an ugly monster that even you turned away from me in disgust? God made humans beautiful like Him, but my form is a hideous reflection of yours, even worse. Satan had his companions, other devils, to be with him and make him feel good about himself. But I am completely alone and hated."

200   These were my thoughts during my sad and lonely times. But when I thought about the good qualities of the people in the small house, how kind and caring they were, I thought they would feel sorry for me and not care about my physical appearance. Could they reject someone, no matter how strange, who asked for their kindness and friendship? I decided that I wouldn't give up hope and would do everything I could to prepare for a meeting with them that would determine my future. I decided to wait a few more months. I wanted to be even more prepared.

201   "Several changes, in the mean time, took place in the cottage. The presence of Safie diffused happiness among its inhabitants. Felix and Agatha were contented and happy. Their feelings were serene and peaceful, while mine became every day more tumultuous. Increase of knowledge only discovered to me more clearly what a wretched outcast I was. I cherished hope, it is true, but it vanished, when I beheld my person reflected in water.

"I endeavoured to crush these fears. However, I was alone. I didn't even have my creator. Where was mine? He had abandoned me and, in the bitterness of my heart, I cursed him.

202   Autumn went by like this. I was surprised and sad to see the leaves wither and fall, and the world become barren and desolate like when I first saw the woods and the beautiful moon. But the cold didn't bother me as much as the heat because of how I was made. My favorite things were the flowers, the birds, and all the bright and cheerful things about summer. When those things were gone, I started paying more attention to the people in the cottages. The absence of summer didn't make them any less happy. They loved each other and cared about each other, and their happiness wasn't affected by the bad things happening around them. The more I saw them, the more I wanted them to protect me and be kind to me. I really wanted them to know me and like me. I couldn't bear the thought of them rejecting and hating me. The poor people who came to their door were never turned away. I did ask for more than just some food and a place to rest. I wanted kindness and understanding, but deep down, I didn't think I was completely undeserving of it.

203   The winter came and the seasons changed since I came to life. My focus now was on my plan to introduce myself to the people who were taking care of me. I thought about different ideas, but I decided that I would enter their house when the old man was alone. I realized that people were most scared of me because of how I looked, not because of my voice. So, I believed that if I could win the old De Lacey's trust and get him to help me, maybe the others would accept me too.

One day, when the sun was shining and the ground was covered in red leaves, Safie, Agatha, and Felix went on a long walk in the countryside. The old man, by his own choice, stayed behind alone in the cottage. After his children left, he picked up his guitar and played several sad but beautiful songs. It was even more beautiful and sad than I had ever heard him play before. At first, he looked happy, but as he played, he became thoughtful and sad. Eventually, he stopped playing and sat there lost in his thoughts.

204 "My heart beat quick. This was the hour and moment of trial, which would decide my hopes or make my fears come true. The servants were gone to a nearby fair. All was silent in and around the cottage. It was an excellent opportunity. However, once I started to move, I suddenly felt so nervous. I took a deep breath of fresh air.

"I knocked. 'Who is there?' said the old man—'Come in.'

"I entered: 'Excuse me,' said I: 'I am travelling and need some rest. Can I sit by your fire?'

"'Enter,' said De Lacey; 'and I will try to help you. My children have gone out and I am blind, so I might not be a great host right now.'

"'Do not trouble yourself. I have food. I just need a place to sit.'

"We sat in silence and finally, the old man addressed me—

"'By your language, stranger, I suppose you are from nearby?— Are you French?'

205 "No, but I learned from a French family. I'm also going to ask some other people I somewhat know to help me."

"Are they Germans?"

"No, they're French. But let's talk about something else. I'm a lonely person. I look around and have no family or friends in the world. These kind people I'm going to see have never met me before and know very little about me. I'm filled with fear because if they reject me, I'll be an outcast forever."

"Don't lose hope. Have faith in your hopes. And if these people are good and kind, don't give up."

"They are kind. They are the best people in the world. I am only a little worried that instead of seeing a caring and friendly person, they might only see a horrible monster."

"That's truly unfortunate. But if you truly haven't done anything wrong, can't you prove them wrong?"

206 "I am scared. I care deeply about these people and have done kind acts for them, but they might think I want to harm them. I want to change their minds about me."

"Where do your friends live?" asked the person.

"They live near here," the old man replied.

The old man paused for a moment and then said, "If you tell me your story without holding anything back, I might be able to help you. I am blind. I also may be poor and far from home, but it would make me truly happy to help someone."

"You are such a kind person! I am grateful for your help. I already feel more hopeful.I am worried they think I've done bad things, but I promise that I have not."

"It's important to be honest. I also have faced tragedy. My family and I have been unfairly accused, so I understand what it is like to suffer."

207 "'How can I thank you, my best and only helper? You're the first person to show me kindness. I'm ready to see my friends now.'

'Can you tell me the names and where these friends live?'

I hesitated. I knew this was the critical moment that would either bring me happiness or take it away. I tried hard to find the strength to answer him, but my efforts drained me. I collapsed onto the chair and started crying. Just then, I heard the footsteps of my younger protectors. Time was running out. I grabbed the old man's hand and pleaded, 'Now is the time! Please save and protect me! You and your family are the friends I'm looking for. Please don't abandon me when I need help the most!'

'Oh my goodness!' the old man exclaimed. 'Who are you?'"

208 "At that instant the cottage door was opened, and Felix, Safie, and Agatha entered. Who can describe their horror when they saw

me? Agatha fainted. Safie, unable to help, rushed out of the cottage. Felix darted forward and struck me violently with a stick. I could have torn him limb from limb, but my heart wa heavy. I escaped to my hovel behind the cottage."

CHAPTER

SIXTEEN

 "I CURSED, cursed creator! Why did I have to live? Why, at that moment, didn't I just end the life you so recklessly gave me? I don't know; despair hadn't taken over yet. I was consumed by rage and a desire for revenge. I would have taken pleasure in destroying the cottage and everyone inside, relishing in their screams and suffering.

When night came, I left my hiding place and wandered through the woods. With no fear of being discovered, I let out my anguish in terrifying howls. I was like a wild animal freed from its trap, destroying anything in my path and moving through the woods with the speed of a deer. Oh, what a miserable night I endured! The cold stars mocked me, and the bare trees swayed their branches above me. Every now and then, a bird's sweet voice broke through the silence. Everyone but me was at peace or enjoying themselves. I, like a devil, carried a hellish torment inside me. Feeling utterly alone and ununderstood, I wanted to uproot the trees, cause chaos and destruction, and then sit back and revel in the ruin.

 "But this was a wonderful feeling that couldn't last. I got tired and overwhelmed. From that moment, I declared a war against all

93

humans, especially the one who created me and forced me into this unbearable suffering.

The sun came up. I heard people talking, and I knew I couldn't go back to my hiding place for the rest of the day. So, I found a hiding spot in some bushes and decided to spend the next few hours thinking about my situation.

The warm sunshine and fresh air of the day brought some calmness back to me; when I thought about what had happened at the cottage, I realized I might have acted too quickly. I had definitely made some mistakes. It was clear that my conversation had made the father interested in helping me, and I was foolish to expose myself to the terror of his children. I should have slowly gained the old De Lacey's trust and eventually revealed myself to the rest of the family when they were ready to meet me. But I didn't believe my mistakes were impossible to fix; after thinking for a long time, I decided to go back to the cottage, find the old man, and try to convince him to join my side."

211 "These thoughts calmed me, and in the afternoon I sank into a profound sleep, but the fever of my blood caused me to have nightmares. Eventually, once night came, I crept forth from my hiding-place, and went in search of food.

"After I ate, I crept into my hovel. Morning came and the inside of the cottage was dark, and I heard no motion. I was so worried. I cannot describe the agony of this suspense.

"Presently two men passed by but I had no idea what they were saying. Soon after, however, Felix approached with another man. I was surprised, as I knew that he had not left the cottage that morning, and waited anxiously to see what was going on.

212 "Do you think," his friend said to him, "that you'll have to pay three months' rent and lose the crops from your garden? I don't want to take advantage of you, so I'm asking you to take some time to think about your decision."

"It's pointless," replied Felix. "We can never live in your cottage again. My father's life is in great danger because of what I've told you. My wife and sister will never recover from the horror. Please don't try to reason with me anymore. Take back your house, and let me leave this place."

Felix trembled as he spoke. He and his friend went into the cottage, where they stayed for a few minutes before leaving. I never saw any of the De Lacey family again.

213 I spent the rest of the day in my small house feeling completely hopeless and stupid. My protectors had left and had broken the only thing connecting me to the world. For the first time, I felt a strong desire for revenge and hatred. I thought of the De Laceys fondly, but again, when I remembered that they had rejected and abandoned me, anger returned, a strong anger. Since I couldn't harm any people, I directed my fury towards objects that couldn't feel anything. As night came, I put various flammable things around the cottage, and after destroying everything in the garden, I impatiently waited for the moon to go down so I could start my plan.

214 As the night got darker, a strong wind blew in from the woods, pushing away the clouds that were hanging in the sky. The gust of wind felt powerful, like a giant avalanche, and it made me feel like I was losing my mind. I found a dry branch from a tree and lit it on fire. I started to dance in a frenzy around the cottage, my eyes fixed on the horizon where the moon was almost touching. Eventually, the moon started to disappear behind the edge, and I waved my burning branch. It sank, and with a loud scream, I set fire to the straw, heath, and bushes I had gathered. The wind blew harder, and the flames quickly surrounded the cottage, licking it with their destructive tongues.

Once I realized that no one could save any part of the house, I left the scene and sought shelter in the nearby woods.

215 "And now, where should I even go? I thought about trying to find you. You had mentioned Geneva as the name of your native town; and towards this place I resolved to proceed.

"But how was I to direct myself? I couldn't think about any of that. I only knew that I had to find you. I needed answers and you needed to give them to me.

216   My journey was long, and I suffered a lot. I left the area where I had been living for a long time in the late autumn. I only traveled at night because I was scared of seeing any other humans. The nature around me was dying. The closer I got to where you lived, the more revengeful I felt. Snow fell and everything became frozen, but I didn't stop. Sometimes, I came across a few things that showed me the way, and I had a map of the area, but I often got lost. I was in so much pain that I couldn't rest. Every little thing that happened fueled my anger and misery. But something that happened when I reached the borders of Switzerland, when the sun started to warm up again and the earth looked green, made my feelings even more bitter and horrifying.

217   I often rested during the day and only traveled at night so that no one would see me. But one morning, as I had to pass through a deep forest, I decided to continue my journey after the sun had already risen. It was one of the first days of spring, and the sunshine and warm air made me feel cheerful, which was quite unusual for me. I was pleasantly surprised by the new emotions of gentleness and happiness that welled up inside me. For a moment, I forgot about my loneliness and appearance, and I allowed myself to be happy. Tears of joy rolled down my cheeks, and I even looked up at the bright sun with gratitude for bringing such happiness to my heart.

218   I kept going through the paths of the wood until I reached its edge, where there was a deep and fast river. Some of the trees leaned over the river with new spring leaves. I didn't know which way to go, so I stopped and heard voices. I decided to hide under a cypress tree. Just then, a young girl ran towards me, laughing as if she was playing a game of chase. She kept running along the steep riverbank and suddenly slipped, falling into the rushing water. Without thinking, I rushed out of my hiding place and used all my strength to save her and bring her to shore. She was unconscious, and I tried everything I could to wake her up. Suddenly, a country person, who was probably

the person she was playing with, came towards us. When he saw me, he grabbed the girl from me and quickly ran deeper into the woods. I followed after them, not sure why. But when he saw me getting closer, he pointed a gun at me and shot. I fell to the ground, and he quickly ran away into the woods.

219   This was the reward for my kindness! I had saved someone's life, and in return, I was now in pain from a deep wound. The feelings of kindness and gentleness I just had were replaced with intense anger and hatred towards all people. The pain overwhelmed me, causing me to faint.

For a few weeks, I lived a miserable life in the woods, trying to heal my wound. I didn't know if the bullet was still inside or if it had gone through. Besides, there was no way for me to remove it. Every day, I swore to get revenge.

After a few weeks, my wound finally healed, and I continued my journey. The hardships I endured could no longer be eased by the warm sun or gentle breeze of spring. Any joy felt like a cruel joke, reminding me of my lonely existence and the fact that I couldn't find happiness.

But my struggles were almost over. In two months, I arrived near Geneva.

220   It was evening when I arrived, so I found a place to hide in the fields that surround the town. I needed time to think about how to approach you. I was tired, hungry, and too sad to appreciate the gentle evening breeze or the view of the sun setting behind the tall Jura mountains.

At that moment, I drifted into a light sleep, finding some relief from my troubled thoughts. However, my rest was interrupted by the arrival of a lovely child who ran into the same hiding spot I had chosen, full of the joyful energy of youth. As I looked at him, an idea struck me – this little child was innocent and hadn't had enough time to develop a fear of deformity. If I could take him and raise him as my companion and friend, perhaps I wouldn't feel so lonely in this crowded world.

Driven by this impulse, I grabbed the boy as he passed by and pulled him towards me. The moment he saw my appearance, he covered his eyes with his hands and let out a high-pitched scream. I forcibly removed his hands from his face and said, "Child, why are you reacting this way? I don't want to harm you; just listen to me."

He fought against my grip and shouted, "Let me go! You monster! Ugly creature! You want to eat me and tear me apart! You're an ogre! Let me go, or I'll tell my dad!"

"Boy, you won't see your father again. You have to come with me," I responded.

"Hideous monster! Let me go! My dad is an important person. He is Mr. Frankenstein, a Syndic. He will punish you. You're not allowed to keep me!"

"Frankenstein! So you belong to my enemy, the one I've sworn to take revenge on forever. You'll be my first victim," the creature declared.

The child kept struggling and insulted me with words that pierced my heart. To quiet him, I gripped his throat, and in an instant, he was lifeless at my feet.

As I looked at my victim, a surge of satisfaction and wicked triumph filled my heart. Clapping my hands together, I exclaimed, "I, too, can cause destruction. My enemy is not invincible. This death will bring despair to him, and countless miseries will torment and destroy him."

While my gaze remained fixed on the child, I noticed something sparkling on his chest. I took it, realizing it was a portrait of a beautiful woman. Despite my evil intent, her image softened and captivated me. For a brief moment, I delighted in her dark eyes framed with long lashes and her lovely lips. But soon, my anger returned. I remembered that I was forever deprived of the happiness that such beautiful creatures could offer. If she saw me, her expression of divine kindness would transform into one of disgust and fear.

Can you imagine the rage that swelled within me upon such thoughts? I marvel only that in that moment, instead of crying out in agony and despair, I didn't rush into the world and perish while attempting to destroy mankind.

222   While I was overwhelmed with these feelings, I left the place where I had done the killing. I looked for a quieter hiding spot and went into an empty barn. Inside, there was a young woman sleeping on some straw. She wasn't as beautiful as the woman in the picture I held, but she had a pleasant face and looked healthy and youthful. I thought to myself, here is someone who shares their joyful smiles with everyone except me. I leaned down towards her and whispered, "Wake up, my dearest. Your lover is here, someone who would give their life just to see a glimmer of affection in your eyes. My beloved, please wake up!"

The sleeper stirred, and fear shot through me. What if she woke up, saw me, and cursed and exposed me as a murderer? That's surely what she would do if her eyes opened and she saw me. The thought drove me mad. It awakened the evil inside of me. I decided that she, not I, should suffer. I committed this murder because I've been robbed of everything I could have had from her, so she should pay for it. Thanks to what I learned from Felix and the harsh laws of society, I now knew how to cause harm. I leaned over her, and carefully placed the portrait into a fold of her dress, making sure it was secure. She stirred again, and I quickly ran away.

223   "For a few days, I kept going back to the place where those things happened. Sometimes, I wanted to see you, and other times, I thought about leaving the world and all its troubles forever. Eventually, I wandered towards these mountains and explored their massive hidden areas while being consumed by a strong desire that only you can fulfill. We can't part ways until you promise to do what I ask. I'm all by myself, feeling miserable because people won't be around me. But someone as disfigured and dreadful as I am wouldn't say no to me. My companion must be of the same kind and have the same flaws. You have to create this being for me."

CHAPTER
SEVENTEEN

224 THE BEING STOPPED TALKING and looked at me, waiting for an answer. But I was confused and couldn't organize my thoughts enough to understand what he was asking. He kept going,

"You have to make a female companion for me. I demand it as something you must give me."

As he finished telling his story, my anger flared up again. I couldn't hold back my rage any longer.

"I refuse," I said firmly. "No amount of torture will ever make me agree. You might make me the most miserable person, but you will never make me feel ashamed of myself. Should I create someone like you, whose evilness could destroy the world? Leave! I have given you my answer. You can try to torture me, but I will never agree."

225 "You're wrong," said the fiend. "Instead of threatening, I want to reason with you. I'm malicious because I'm miserable. Everyone shuns and hates me, including you, my creator. You would tear me apart and feel triumphant. Remember that and tell me why I should pity humans when they don't pity me? You wouldn't call it murder if you could throw me into one of those ice cracks and destroy the body you made. Should I respect humans when they despise me? Let's live

"""

together with kindness, and instead of hurting each other, I would give you every benefit with tears of gratitude when you accept them. But that can't happen since our different senses make it impossible for us to unite. I won't be a slave to anyone. I will have revenge for what you've done to me. If I can't inspire love, I will make people fear me. And I will direct most of that fear towards you, my arch-enemy, because you're my creator. I swear to you that I will hate you forever. Be careful: I will work to destroy you and won't stop until I crush your heart, so you'll regret the day you were born."

A ferocious anger consumed him as he spoke; his face contorted in a way too terrifying for any person to witness. But soon he regained his composure and continued—

"I wanted to reason with you. This intense emotion is harmful to me, but you don't realize that you are the reason for its intensity. If anyone ever showed kindness towards me, I would return it a hundred times over. For that one person, I would make peace with everyone! But now I'm only dreaming of a happiness I can never have. What I ask of you is fair and reasonable: I want a companion. I know we would be rejected by society, but that would only make us more attached to each other. Our lives won't be happy, but they would be free from the misery. Please don't deny me."

I was deeply affected. The thought of what might happen if I agreed made me tremble, but there was some truth in his argument. His story and his current feelings showed that he was capable of experiencing deep emotions. As his creator, didn't I owe him whatever happiness I could give? He noticed my change of heart and kept speaking-

"If you agree, we will never be seen by you or any other human again. I will go to the vast wilderness of South America. I don't eat the same food as humans. Acorns and berries give me enough nourishment. My companion will be like me and will be satisfied with the same food. We will sleep on dried leaves. We won't need much. Even though you have been cruel to me, I can see compassion in your eyes now. Let me take this opportunity to persuade you to promise me what I desperately desire."

"You suggest," I replied, "that you should run away and live in the wilderness where only animals will be your companions. How can you, who long for human love and understanding, continue with this exile? You will come back and seek their kindness again, but they will hate you. Your evil desires will return, and then you will have a companion to help you cause destruction. That cannot happen. Please stop arguing, as I cannot agree to your request."

228 "How quickly your feelings change! Just a moment ago, you were moved by what I said, so why are you now hardening your heart? I promise you, on the earth I live on and by the one who created me, that if you give me a companion, I will leave human society and live wherever I can, even in the wildest places. My evil desires will fade because I'll have company. I will not curse the one who made me."

His words had a strange effect on me. I felt sorry for him. I thought that since I couldn't feel the same way he did, I had no right to deny him the small amount of happiness I could offer.

"You promise," I said, "to be harmless, but haven't you already shown some spite that makes it reasonable for me to distrust you? Couldn't this all be a trick to increase your satisfaction by allowing you to seek even more revenge?"

229 "What's going on? I won't be treated lightly, and I want an answer. If I have no connections or love in my life, then I'll be filled with hatred and vice. Only the love of another will stop me from committing crimes, and I'll become someone who no one knows exists. My bad behaviors come from the loneliness I hate, and my good qualities will naturally emerge when I'm in the company of an equal. I'll experience emotions like any sensitive person and be a part of the chain of life and events from which I'm currently excluded."

I took a long pause to think about everything he had said and the arguments he had made. I considered the promise of virtues. I also thought about his power and threats: a creature who could survive in icy caves and hide in unreachable cliffs would have abilities that couldn't be easily dealt with. After a deep moment of thought, I decided that justice, for him and for my fellow humans, required me to grant his request. Turning towards him, I finally said—

230   "I agree to your request, but you must promise on oath to leave Europe and any other places near humans forever. Once I give you a female companion for your exile, you must keep your promise," I told him.

He exclaimed, "I swear it. You will never see me again as long as they are alive. Go back to your home and start your preparations. I will anxiously watch their progress and when you are ready, I will show up."

After saying this, he quickly left me, perhaps worried that my feelings might change. I watched him swiftly descend the mountain, moving faster than an eagle in flight, and soon he disappeared among the icy waves of the sea."

231   His story had taken all day, and it was almost sunset when he left. I felt bad as I thought about him making his way to wherever he was going. I cried a lot and held my hands together in anguish. "Oh, stars and clouds and wind," I said, "If you really feel sorry for me, take away my feelings and memories and make me disappear. But if you won't, then go away, go away, and leave me in the darkness."

These were crazy and miserable thoughts.

232   I arrived at the village of Chamounix in the morning, but I didn't take any rest. Instead, I immediately went back to Geneva. I couldn't find the words to express how I felt, as my emotions were overwhelming and burdened me like a heavy mountain. So, I returned home and went inside the house to be with my family. They were deeply alarmed by my tired looks, but I didn't answer any questions and hardly spoke. I was totally lost in thoughts of what I had to do next.

CHAPTER

EIGHTEEN

233   I SPENT many days and weeks back in Geneva, but I couldn't find the courage to start working again. I was afraid of the revenge of the disappointed monster, and I didn't want to do the task I was given. To create a female being, I needed to study and research for several more months. I heard about an English scientist who made some important discoveries that could help me, and I thought about asking my father if I could go to England for that reason. But I kept finding excuses to delay, and I didn't want to take the first step in a task that didn't feel so urgent anymore. Something had changed in me: my health had gotten better, and my spirits were higher when I wasn't thinking about my unhappy promise. My father was happy to see this change, and he tried to find ways to help me get rid of my sadness, which sometimes returned and made everything seem dark again. During those moments, I found solace in being completely alone. I would spend whole days on the lake in a small boat, looking at the clouds and listening to the sounds of the waves. It made me feel calm and peaceful. And when I came back, I would greet my friends with a warmer smile and a happier heart.

234   After coming back from one of my walks, my father asked to talk

104

to me privately. He said, "I'm glad to see that you're enjoying your old pleasures again and starting to be yourself. But you're still unhappy and avoiding being with us. I've been trying to figure out why. What's going on with you?"

I was really scared by how he started, and my father continued, saying, "I admit that I've always thought that you and Elizabeth would get married and bring happiness to our home. You two have been close since you were babies, studying together and having similar interests. But sometimes people don't see things clearly. What I thought would help my plan may have actually ruined it. Maybe you see Elizabeth only as a sister and don't want to marry her. Perhaps you've met someone else you love, and you feel trapped because of your commitment to Elizabeth. This struggle might be causing the strong sadness you're showing."

"Dear father, please don't worry. I truly and deeply love my cousin. Elizabeth is the only woman who has ever made me feel such strong admiration and affection. I can't imagine my future without the hope of marrying her."

"Your words bring me great joy, my dear Victor. If you feel this way, then we will surely find happiness together, no matter what challenges we face. But I sense that something is troubling you deeply. Please tell me if you have any concerns about getting married right away. We have faced unfortunate events recently, which have disrupted the peace we used to have. I am older, and I understand that you have a good amount of money. Getting married early shouldn't interfere with any future plans you may have for success and doing good in the world. However, I don't want to force happiness on you, and if you need more time, it won't cause me serious worry. Please understand my intentions and honestly tell me your thoughts and feelings."

I listened quietly to my father and couldn't respond for a while. My mind quickly spun with many thoughts as I tried to make a decision. But oh, the idea of marrying Elizabeth right away was horrifying and filled me with dread. I had made a solemn promise that I hadn't fulfilled yet, and I couldn't break it. If I did, so many terrible things could happen to me and my loving family. How could I go to a celebration burdened by this heavy weight around my neck, dragging me down? I had to keep my promise and let the monster go with his partner before I could find peace in the happiness of our marriage.

237 I also remembered that I had to either go to England or communicate with philosophers from there to get the knowledge and discoveries I needed for my current project. The second option, writing letters back and forth, was slow and unsatisfying. Plus, I really didn't want to be stuck doing my disgusting task in my dad's house while being around the people I cared about. I knew that so many things could go wrong, even the smallest mishap could reveal the horrifying truth to everyone close to me. I needed to be alone so I could work. After fulfilling my promise, the monster would be gone forever. Or maybe (if I allowed myself to imagine), something might happen to him and free me from being his slave forever.

238 I told my father my feelings and asked if I could go to England. I didn't reveal the true reasons behind my request, but instead, I made it seem like I just wanted to go on a trip for fun. He agreed.

He let me decide how long I wanted to stay there, allowing a few months or maybe a year at the most. He also made sure I wouldn't be alone during my journey. Without telling me in advance, he and Elizabeth arranged for my friend, Clerval, to go with me. I was glad, but also a little worried. I needed to really focus. But, Henry's presence might prevent my enemy from bothering me. If I were alone, wouldn't he sometimes force himself into my life, reminding me of my job or watching me work?

239 I was determined to go to England, and it was understood that when I returned, I would marry Elizabeth right away. My father, being older, didn't want any delays.

I started making plans for my journey, but one fear kept troubling me. What would happen to my friends while I was away? They didn't know about our enemy and wouldn't be protected from his attacks. He had promised to follow me wherever I went, so would he come with me to England? This thought was terrifying, but at the same time, it gave me some comfort, as it meant my friends would be safe. I was tormented by the possibility that the opposite might happen. However, in all the time I was under the control of my creation, I let my impulses guide me, and my current feelings strongly suggested that the monster would follow me and spare my family from his evil schemes.

240   In late September, I left my home again. It was my idea to go on this journey, and Elizabeth agreed, even though she worried about me being away. She wanted me to hurry back, but she couldn't find the words to express all her mixed emotions when we tearfully said goodbye.

    I climbed into the carriage, not really sure where I was headed and not paying attention to what was happening around me. I had all of my tools with me. Even though I knew the road to where I was going would be beautiful, all I could think about was my task ahead.

241   After a few lazy days, during which I traveled a long way, I arrived in Strasburgh. I waited there for two days for Clerval. Finally, he came. But oh, how different we were! He was excited about each new sight. He was joyful when he saw the beautiful sunset and even happier when he saw the sunrise and a new day. Honestly, I was consumed by dark thoughts. I didn't notice the evening star or the golden sunrise. He looked at the scenery with a sense of emotion and excitement, unlike my own reflections. I am just a miserable person, doomed to suffer and unable to find any happiness.

242   We had planned to take a boat trip down the Rhine from Strasburgh to Rotterdam, where we would then board a ship to London. During this journey, we passed many small islands covered in willow trees and saw some beautiful towns along the way. We stopped for a day in Manheim, and on the fifth day since leaving Strasburgh, we arrived at Mayence. Below Mayence, the Rhine takes on a more picturesque setting. The river flows rapidly and winds its way between hills that may not be very tall, but have lovely shapes. We

saw many old castles in ruins perched on the edges of steep cliffs, surrounded by dark forests that are high and unreachable. This part of the Rhine offers a unique and ever-changing landscape. In one place, you can see rugged hills, castle ruins towering over steep cliffs, with the deep Rhine River flowing below. Then, as you turn a corner, you are greeted by flourishing vineyards on a promontory, with green sloping banks and a winding river, along with lively towns bustling with people.

243   We traveled during the grape harvest time and heard the workers singing as we floated down the river. Even though I was feeling down and had gloomy thoughts, I still felt happy. I lay at the bottom of the boat and looked up at the clear blue sky, feeling a peace I hadn't felt in a long time. And if I felt that way, imagine how Henry felt. He thought he had been transported to a magical place and was experiencing a happiness that's rare for people. "I have seen," he said, "the most beautiful sights in my own country. I've been to Lake Lucerne and Lake Uri, where the snowy mountains go straight down into the water, creating dark shadows that could be gloomy and sad if it weren't for the lush green islands that brighten everything up. I've seen storms on the lake, with the wind making whirlwinds of water, giving us a glimpse of what a waterspout is like on the big ocean. The waves crash violently against the mountain base where a priest and his lover were buried by an avalanche. They say you can still hear their voices in the night wind. I've seen the mountains in Valais and Vaud, but this place, Victor, is more pleasing to me than all those wonders. The Swiss mountains are bigger and more strange, but there's something special about the banks of this amazing river that I've never seen anywhere else. Look at that castle hanging over the cliff and the one on the island, hidden among the trees' green leaves. Now look at the group of workers coming from their vineyards and the village tucked away in the mountain's nook. Oh, for sure, the spirit that lives here and protects this place understands and connects more with humans than those who climb glaciers or hide on the top of our own country's unreachable peaks."

244   Clerval! Dear friend! I am so happy to write down your words now and think about the compliments you truly deserve. You were like a character from a beautiful poem, created by nature itself. Your wild and imaginative thoughts were balanced by your sensitive heart. You had so much love in your soul, and your friendship was so deep and amazing that people say it can only exist in stories. But even though you had deep connections with others, it wasn't enough for your curious mind. You had a fiery passion for the natural world that others only appreciated, but you truly loved:

"The loud waterfall was like an obsession to you. The tall rocks, mountains, and dark woods with all their colors and shapes were more than just sights to you. They were like food for your soul, something to feel and love deeply. You didn't need anything more, like thoughts or other interests, to make them even more special. Just looking at them with your own eyes was enough."

And now, where are you? Is this gentle and lovely person gone forever? Has this brilliant mind, full of creative ideas and grand thoughts that formed a whole world, a world that only existed because of its creator's life—has this mind disappeared? Does it only exist in my memories now? No, that's not true. Your body, beautifully made and radiant, may have decayed, but your spirit still visits and comforts your sad friend.

245   Excuse my sorrow. I miss Henry very much. I will proceed with my tale.

Beyond Cologne we descended to the plains of Holland.

Our journey here lost the interest arising from beautiful scenery; but we arrived in a few days at Rotterdam, whence we proceeded by sea to England. It was on a clear morning, in the latter days of December, that I first saw the white cliffs of Britain. The banks of the Thames presented a new scene. They were flat, but fertile, and almost every town was marked by the remembrance of some story. So much history.

CHAPTER

NINETEEN

246 LONDON WAS where we decided to rest for a while. We planned to stay here for several months in this amazing and famous city. Clerval wanted to meet and spend time with talented and intelligent people who were thriving at that time. But for me, that was not the main goal. I was primarily focused on finding the information I needed to fulfill my promise. I quickly took advantage of the letters of introduction I had brought with me. These letters were addressed to the most well-known scientists.

If this journey had happened during my days of studying and being happy, it would have brought me immense joy. But my life had been affected by a terrible tragedy, and now I only visited these people to gather the information I desperately needed. Being around other people was difficult for me. When I was alone, I could lose myself in the wonders of the world around me. Henry's voice comforted me, and for a brief moment, I could fool myself into feeling at peace. But seeing busy, uninteresting, and happy faces only brought back my despair. I felt like there was an insurmountable barrier between myself and other people. This barrier was stained with the blood of William and Justine. Thinking about the events connected to those names filled me with sorrow.

In Clerval, I saw a reflection of my past self. He was curious and eager to learn. He found the differences in manners to be fascinating and entertaining. He was always busy, and the only thing that dampened his enjoyment was my sadness. I tried my best to hide it, so I wouldn't prevent him from experiencing the joys of starting a new chapter in life without any worries or painful memories. Many times, I turned down his invitations, claiming other obligations, so I could be alone. At that time, I also started gathering the materials I needed for my new creation. It felt like being tortured, drop by drop, every time I thought about it. Even mentioning it made my lips tremble and my heart beat faster.

After spending a few months in London, we got a letter from someone in Scotland who had visited us when we were in Geneva. They talked about how beautiful their home country was and invited us to go as far north as Perth, where they lived. Clerval really wanted to go, and even though I didn't like being around people, I wanted to see mountains and streams again, and all the amazing things that Nature creates in those places.

We arrived in England in October, and now it was February. We decided that we would start our journey to the north at the end of the next month. Instead of taking the main road to Edinburgh, we planned to visit Windsor, Oxford, Matlock, and the lakes in Cumberland. We wanted to finish this trip by the end of July. I packed up my chemistry tools and the things I had collected, planning to finish my work in a quiet spot in the highlands of Scotland.

On March 27th, we left London and stayed in Windsor for a few days. We explored its beautiful forest, which was new for us from the mountains. The big oak trees, the abundance of animals, and the groups of graceful deer were all things we had never seen before.

We then went to Oxford. When we arrived in the city, we couldn't help but think about the important things that happened here more than 150 years ago. This was where Charles I gathered his army. Oxford stayed loyal to him even when the rest of the country joined the parliament's side for freedom. Remembering that unfortunate king and his companions - Falkland, Goring, his queen, and son - made every part of the city feel special, as if they once lived there. The city itself was beautiful enough to capture our attention, even without those sentimental feelings. The colleges were old and picturesque, and the streets were impressive. The lovely Isis River flowed alongside the city, surrounded by beautiful green meadows. The calm waters reflected the majestic towers, spires, and domes, which looked like they were nestled among old trees.

250   I really liked this scene, but my enjoyment was made less joyful by remembering the past and thinking about the future. I was meant to be happy and at peace. When I was young, I never felt unhappy, and if I ever felt bored, looking at the beauty in nature or studying amazing things created by humans always made me feel better. But now I feel broken, like a tree that's been hit by lightning. I knew then that I would survive, but I would become something pitiful and unbearable.

We spent a good amount of time in Oxford, exploring the areas around it and trying to find places that were important during a really exciting time in English history. Our little adventures often took longer than expected because we kept finding interesting things. For a second, I dared to feel free and brave again. But the pain had taken hold of me, and I went back to being scared and hopeless.

251   We left Oxford feeling a little sad, and went to Matlock, our next place to stay. The area around the village looked a bit like Switzerland, but it was smaller and didn't have the big white mountains in the distance. We went to see a cave and a small museum with interesting things from nature. It reminded me of the collections in Servox and Chamounix. The mention of Chamounix scared me because of what happened there, so I quickly left Matlock because of that memory.

From Derby, we continued north and spent two months in Cumberland and Westmorland. It almost felt like I was in the Swiss mountains. The patches of snow on the mountains, the lakes, and the rushing streams felt familiar and special to me. We also made some friends who made me almost forget about my troubles and made me happy. Clerval, especially, loved being around talented people and discovered new things about himself. He said to me, "I could live here forever and hardly miss Switzerland and the Rhine."

But he discovered that being a traveler involves a lot of both pleasure and pain. His emotions are always in a state of tension. Just when he starts to relax, he realizes he has to leave the place where he was enjoying himself and move on to something new. This new thing captures his attention, but then he leaves that behind for more new experiences.

We had recently explored the lakes in Cumberland and Westmorland and started to become fond of some of the people who lived there. However, it was time for us to meet our friend from Scotland, so we had to leave and continue our journey. Personally, I wasn't too upset about leaving. I had been neglecting a promise I made, and I was afraid of how the creature would react to being let down. I worried that it might stay in Switzerland and seek revenge on my family. This thought haunted me and made it difficult to find any rest or peace. I anxiously awaited my letters, fearing the worst if they were delayed. When they finally arrived, and I saw that they were from Elizabeth or my father, I was almost too scared to read them and find out what would happen to me. Sometimes I believed that the creature was following me, ready to harm my companion as punishment for my mistakes. During these moments, I stuck by Henry's side like a shadow, trying to protect him from the imagined rage of our enemy. It felt as if I had done something terribly wrong, even though I was innocent. But I had brought upon myself a terrible curse, just as real as if I had committed a crime.

I went to Edinburgh feeling tired and uninterested. But even the most unfortunate person would have found that city interesting. Clerval didn't like it as much as Oxford because he preferred the city's oldness. However, the beauty and orderliness of Edinburgh's new town, its romantic castle, and the amazing places nearby like Arthur's Seat, St. Bernard's Well, and the Pentland Hills, made up for the change and filled him with happiness and awe. But I was eager to reach the end of my journey.

We left Edinburgh a week later and traveled through Coupar, St. Andrew's, and along the banks of the Tay River to Perth, where our friend was waiting for us. But I wasn't in the mood to chat and socialize with strangers or to understand their feelings and plans like a good guest should. So, I told Clerval that I wanted to explore Scotland on my own. "You," I said, "have fun and let's meet up here. I might be gone for a month or two, so please don't try to control what I do. Give me some time alone in peace and quiet. I hope that when I come back, I'll have a happier heart that matches your own."

255   Henry tried to convince me otherwise, but I was determined to go ahead with my plan. He begged me to keep in touch through letters. He said, "I'd rather be with you on your solitary walks than with these Scottish people I don't know. Hurry back, my dear friend, so I can feel a sense of home once more. I can't do that when you're not here."

Once I said goodbye to Henry, I made up my mind to visit a remote part of Scotland and complete my work alone. I was certain that the monster was following me and would reveal himself once I finished, so that we could be together.

With this decision in mind, I journeyed through the northern highlands and chose one of the farthest Orkney Islands as my place of work. It was the perfect setting for my task. It was all off on its own.

256   On the entire island, there were only three rundown huts, and one of them was empty when I arrived. I rented it and found it to be in a terrible condition. The roof was falling apart, the walls were bare, and the door was broken. I had it repaired, bought some furniture, and moved in. This surprising event didn't cause much stir among the cottagers, as they were too numb from poverty and need. They hardly noticed or bothered me, and they didn't show much

gratitude when I offered them food and clothes. Suffering has a way of numbing even the strongest emotions.

In this secret place, I worked during the mornings. And when the weather allowed, I walked along the rocky beach to listen to the roaring waves. It was a repetitive yet constantly changing sight. I thought about Switzerland, a far cry from the desolate and scary landscape I was in.

257 In this way, I divided my time when I first got here. But as I continued my work, it became more and more terrible and tiring for me. Sometimes I couldn't bring myself to go into my lab for days, and other times I worked day and night to finish what I was doing. It was a messy process that I was involved in. During my first experiment, I was so caught up in the excitement that I didn't think about how horrifying my job was. I was focused on completing my work and ignored the horror of what I was doing. But now I approached it with a clear mind, and often felt disgusted by what I was doing.

In this unpleasant situation, doing the most awful work and surrounded by solitude where nothing could distract my attention from what I was doing, my mood became uneven. I became restless and anxious. Every moment, I was afraid of running into the person who was pursuing me. Sometimes I sat with my eyes fixed on the ground, afraid to look up in case I saw the person I dreaded. I was afraid to be alone, in case he showed up to claim me.

Meanwhile, I continued to work, and I had already made a lot of progress. I looked forward to finishing it with a shaky and eager hope that I couldn't bring myself to question. But at the same time, there was this feeling of something bad on the horizon that made me sick to my stomach.

CHAPTER
TWENTY

258   ONE EVENING, I was sitting in my laboratory. The sun had set and the moon was just rising from the sea. I didn't have enough light for my work, so I took a break to think about whether I should stop for the night or continue until I finished. As I sat there, I started to reflect on the consequences of what I was doing. Three years ago, I was doing the same thing and created a monster who brought so much pain and regret to my life. Now, I was about to create another being, but I had no idea what it would be like. This new creature could be even more evil than its mate, finding pleasure in causing harm and suffering. While the male creature had promised to stay away from humans and hide in deserts, the female might not make the same promise. She, who would become a thinking and reasoning being, might refuse to obey the agreement made before she existed. They might even hate each other. The creature that already existed despised its own ugliness, so could it develop an even stronger hatred when faced with a female version of itself? She might also reject him and be attracted to the beauty of humans. She could leave him, and he would be alone again, feeling even more angry and hurt because another of his kind had abandoned him.

259 Even if they were to leave Europe and live in the deserts of a new land, there would still be consequences to the desires of the monster. They would have children, and these devilish offspring could make life dangerous and uncertain for all humans. Was it right for me to bring this curse upon future generations for my own benefit? I used to be convinced by the persuasive arguments of the monster I created, and his horrifying threats left me speechless.

I trembled and my heart sank when I looked up and saw the monster at the window by the light of the moon. His lips curled into a terrifying grin. Now, he had come to observe my progress and demand that I fulfill my promise.

260 As I looked at him, he had an extremely malicious and deceitful expression on his face. I thought about my promise to create another creature like him, and I was overcome with anger and fear. In a fit of passion, I angrily tore apart the thing I was working on. The monster saw me destroy the creature that he depended on for his future happiness. He let out a howl of despair and revenge, and then he left.

I left the room and locked the door behind me. I made a promise to myself that I would never continue my work again. I went to my room.

Several hours went by, and I stayed by my window, looking out at the sea. It was calm and still. I could feel the silence around me, although I didn't fully realize how deep and profound it was. Suddenly, my attention was captured by the sound of oars splashing near the shore, and I saw someone arriving at my house.

261 In just a few minutes, I heard the squeaking of my door, as if someone was trying to open it quietly. I shook with fear, sensing who it might be. I wanted to wake up one of the nearby villagers who lived in a cottage not far from mine. But I felt completely powerless, like in those scary dreams where you try to run away from danger but can't move.

Soon, I heard footsteps coming down the hallway. The door opened, and the creature I dreaded stood before me. He closed the door and came closer, speaking with a muffled voice.

"You destroyed the thing you started. What do you plan to do now? Are you really going to break your promise? I've endured so much hardship and suffering. I traveled with you from Switzerland, and crossed the Rhine, passing its islands and hills. I spent many months in the English moors and Scottish deserts. I've endured so much fatigue, cold, and hunger. Will you really destroy all my hopes?"

"Go away! I am breaking my promise. I will never create another creature like you, so horrifying and evil."

"Slave, I tried reasoning with you before, but you have shown that you don't deserve my kindness. Remember, I have power. You may think you're miserable now, but I can make you so unhappy that you'll despise the daylight. You may have created me, but I am your master. Obey me!"

262   "The time for my indecisiveness is over, and now you have power over me. Your threats won't make me do something wicked; instead, they only strengthen my determination not to create a companion for you in evil. Should I release a monster into the world, who finds joy in death and misery? Go away! I am resolute, and your words will only make me angrier."

The creature could see my determination on my face and became furious, gnashing his teeth in helplessness. "Should every man find a wife, and every animal find a mate, while I am left alone? I had feelings of love, but they were met with hate and rejection. Human! You might hate, but be careful! Your hours will be filled with fear and misery, and soon a disaster will strike, taking away your happiness forever. Will you be happy while I suffer deeply? You may destroy my other emotions, but revenge remains – revenge, now more important to me than anything. I may die, but before I do, you, my oppressor and tormentor, will curse the sun for witnessing your misery. Be warned, for I am brave and therefore strong. I will watch you like a cunning snake, ready to strike with its venom. Human, you will regret the harm you cause."

"Devil, stop! Don't fill the air with these malicious words. I have made my decision clear to you, and I am not a coward who will yield to mere words. Leave me; I am unyielding."

"Alright, I understand. I will leave, but remember, I will be with you on the night of your wedding."

I quickly moved forward and shouted, "Criminal! Before you seal my fate, make sure that you are safe yourself."

I would have grabbed hold of him, but he slipped away from me and left the house in a hurry. In just a few moments, I saw him in his boat, racing across the water and soon disappearing into the waves.

Everything became quiet once again, but his words echoed in my ears. I burned with anger at the thought of chasing after the one who destroyed my happiness and throwing him into the ocean. I paced back and forth in my room, feeling restless and disturbed, while my mind conjured up countless tormenting images. Why hadn't I followed him and engaged in a fight to the death? However, I had let him go, and he had headed towards the mainland. It horrified me to think about who might be the next victim targeted by his never-ending revenge. And then, his words echoed in my mind again, "I will be with you on your wedding-night." That would be the time when my destiny would be fulfilled. In that hour, I would die, meeting both his cruelty and ending it. The thought didn't make me afraid, but when I considered my beloved Elizabeth—her tears and endless sorrow when she discovered her lover cruelly snatched away from her—tears, the first I had shed in months, streamed down my face, and I vowed not to go down without a bitter fight against my enemy."

As the night faded and the sun came up from the sea, my emotions became a little calmer, although it's hard to call it calm when rage turns into despair. I left the house, the terrible place where last night's argument took place, and strolled along the beach. I saw the sea as a barrier that kept me apart from others, and for a moment, I even wished it was true. I wished to spend my life on that lonely rock just to avoid any more sudden misery.

I had been awake all night, my nerves were frazzled, and my eyes were sore from exhaustion and sorrow. The sleep that enveloped me brought some refreshment, and when I woke up, I felt, once again, like I belonged to the human race. I started thinking about what had happened with a little more calmness. Still, the monster's words echoed in my ears, like the sound of death, feeling like a dream but also a heavy reality.

265   The sun was going down, and I was still sitting on the shore, eating a simple cake, desperately hungry. Then, a fishing boat came ashore near me, and one of the men gave me a package. It had letters from Geneva, and one from my friend Clerval, asking me to join him. He said he was wasting his time where he was and that his friends in London wanted him to come back so they could continue their business deal in India. He couldn't wait any longer to leave, and he wanted me to come with him. He asked me to leave my lonely island and meet him in Perth, so we could travel south together. This letter gave me a bit of hope, and I decided that I would leave the island in two days.

266   But before I left, there was something I dreaded having to do: I needed to pack up my chemical tools. That meant I had to go into the room where I had done my terrible work and touch those instruments that made me feel sick just by looking at them. The next morning, as soon as it was light outside, I gathered my courage and unlocked the door to my laboratory. The pieces of the creature I had been building but destroyed were scattered on the floor. It was as if I had hurt a real person. I took a moment to compose myself and then went inside. With my hands shaking, I moved the instruments out of the room. But I knew I couldn't leave the evidence of what I had done for the villagers to find and fear. So, I put the instruments in a basket with a lot of rocks. I planned to throw them into the sea that very night. In the meantime, I sat on the beach, cleaning and organizing my chemical tools.

267   Nothing could be more complete than the change in my feelings since the night the monster appeared. Before, I saw my promise as something I had to do, no matter what. But now, it's like a veil has

been lifted from my eyes and I can see clearly. I never even thought about continuing my work. The warning I heard kept playing in my mind, but I didn't consider that I could do anything to prevent it. I had decided that creating another monster like the first would be a horribly selfish and wicked act. I pushed away any thoughts that might lead me to think otherwise.

268 Around two or three in the morning, the moon started to rise. I gathered my things and got on a small boat, sailing about four miles away from shore. It was completely quiet and empty. A few boats were coming back to land, but I went in the opposite direction. I felt like I was about to do something terrible, so I didn't want to come across anyone else. Suddenly, the moon, which had been clear, disappeared behind a thick cloud. It was dark, and I took the opportunity to throw my basket into the sea. I listened to the sound of it sinking and then sailed away. The sky got cloudy, but the air was still fresh and cool from the breeze coming from the northeast. It made me feel better and gave me a pleasant feeling, so I decided to stay out on the water longer. I set the rudder in a straight position and lay down at the bottom of the boat. With the moon hidden and everything dark, all I could hear was the sound of the boat gliding through the waves. That sound calmed me, and before I knew it, I was fast asleep.

269 I'm not sure how long I slept, but when I woke up, I saw that the sun was already high up in the sky. The wind was strong, and the waves kept splashing into my small boat, making me worried. I realized that the wind was blowing from the northeast and had probably carried me far away from the coast where I started. I tried to change my direction, but the boat would quickly fill with water if I tried. So, my only option was to let the wind push me along. I have to admit, I felt a bit scared. I didn't have a compass with me, and I didn't know this area very well, so the sun wasn't much help. I could end up in the vast Atlantic Ocean, suffering from hunger and thirst, or be swallowed by the enormous waves around me. I had already been out for many hours, and I was starting to feel very thirsty, which was just

the beginning of my troubles. I looked up at the cloudy sky, and it seemed like the clouds were running away from the wind, only to be replaced by more clouds. I looked at the sea, and it felt like it was going to be my watery grave. "Monster," I cried, "you've already completed your evil plan!" I thought about Elizabeth, my father, and Clerval, all left behind and at the mercy of the monster's vicious and merciless desires. This idea filled me with such despair and fear, that even now, as the end is near, I tremble just thinking about it.

270 After several hours, the wind calmed down and the sea became peaceful. I started feeling sick and weak from exhaustion, but then I spotted some land to the south.

Even though I was worn out and had been through hours of uncertainty, the sudden realization that I might survive filled me with overwhelming happiness and made me cry.

It's remarkable how our emotions can change so quickly and how even in the midst of suffering, we hold on tightly to our love for life! Using a part of my clothing, I made another sail and eagerly steered towards the land. It appeared rugged and rocky at first, but as I got closer, I could see signs of human habitation. There were boats near the shore, and I felt a sense of relief being back near civilization. I followed the curves of the land closely and spotted a church steeple coming into view behind a small hill. Since I was extremely weak, I decided to head straight for the town, hoping to find nourishment there. Luckily, I had some money with me. As I rounded the hill, I was greeted by a small, tidy town and a welcoming harbor. I entered the harbor with a heart full of joy and gratitude for my unexpected escape.

271 As I was busy working on the boat and getting the sails ready, a few people gathered around. They looked surprised to see me, but instead of offering help, they whispered to each other and made gestures that would have made me a little worried at any other time. But since I was focused on the task at hand, I just noticed that they were speaking English. So, I spoke to them in English and asked,

"Excuse me, can you please tell me the name of this town and where I am?"

"You'll find out soon enough," replied a man with a rough voice. "Maybe you've come to a place that you won't like very much, but you won't have any say in where you stay, I assure you."

I was very surprised to receive such a rude answer from a stranger, and I felt uncomfortable seeing the angry faces of his companions. "Why are you speaking to me so harshly?" I responded. "Surely it's not the way English people treat strangers."

"I don't know," said the man, "what the English custom is, but it's the Irish custom to dislike scoundrels."

As the strange conversation continued, more and more people joined the crowd. Their faces showed a mix of curiosity and anger, which bothered me and made me somewhat worried. I asked for directions to the inn, but no one answered. So, I decided to keep moving forward. The crowd followed me and surrounded me, causing a murmur to rise among them. Then, a shady-looking man came up to me and tapped me on the shoulder. He said, "Come on, sir, you have to come with me to see Mr. Kirwin and explain yourself."

"Who is Mr. Kirwin? Why do I have to explain myself? Isn't this a free country?" I questioned.

"Yes, sir, it's free enough for honest people. Mr. Kirwin is a magistrate, and you need to explain what happened to a man who was found murdered here last night."

This answer startled me, but I quickly composed myself. I knew I was innocent and could easily prove it. So, I followed the man silently and was taken to one of the nicest houses in town. I was exhausted and hungry, but since I was surrounded by a crowd, I made sure to summon all my strength. I didn't want anyone to interpret my fatigue as fear or guilt. Little did I know at that moment the terrible fate that awaited me, which would soon engulf me in horror and despair, erasing any fear of shame or death.

I need to pause here, as it takes a lot of courage to remember the terrifying events that I'm about to recount in detail.

CHAPTER
TWENTY-ONE

I WAS QUICKLY TAKEN to meet the magistrate, an old kind man with gentle ways. He looked at me with a slightly stern expression. Then, he turned to the people who brought me and asked who would be giving their account as witnesses.

Around six men stepped forward. One of them was chosen by the magistrate to speak. He said that he had been fishing the night before with his son and brother-in-law, Daniel Nugent. At about ten o'clock, they noticed a strong wind coming from the north, so they decided to head back to the port. Since it was a very dark night without the moon, they didn't dock at the harbor but instead went to a smaller area about two miles away. The man walked ahead carrying some fishing gear, while the others followed behind. As he was walking on the sand, he accidentally tripped over something and fell down. His companions hurried over to help, and using their lantern, they saw that he had fallen on top of a man who looked dead. They initially thought it might be the body of someone who had drowned and washed ashore, but upon closer inspection, they realized that the clothes were dry and the body was not cold. They brought the body to an old woman's cottage nearby, hoping to revive him, but their efforts were in vain. The young man appeared to be handsome and around twenty-five years old. It seemed like he had been strangled since there were finger marks on his neck.

275   The first part of what this person said didn't really interest me. But when they mentioned the finger marks, it reminded me of my brother's murder and I started feeling really upset. My legs started shaking, and my vision got blurry. I had a bad feeling and when the magistrate saw me, I could tell her was already thinking something awful.

Next, the son confirmed what his father said. Then Daniel Nugent was called to testify. He swore that right before his friend fell, he saw a boat with only one person in it, not far from the shore. And from what he could see in the light of a few stars, he believed it was the same boat I had just come from.

A woman who lived near the beach gave her testimony too. She said that about an hour before she heard about the body being found, she saw a boat with only one person in it leaving from the part of the shore where they later found the body.

Another woman confirmed what the fishermen had said about bringing the body into her house. It wasn't cold yet when they put it in a bed and tried to revive it. Daniel went to get a doctor, but it was too late. The person had already died.

276   A few other men were questioned about my arrival. They agreed that because of the strong north wind that had come up during the night, it was likely that I had been sailing around for a long time and ended up back where I started. They also noticed that the body seemed to have been brought from somewhere else, and because I didn't seem to know the area, it was possible that I had pulled into the harbor without realizing how far away the town of * * * was from where I had left the body.

After hearing this testimony, Mr. Kirwin decided to have me taken to the room where the body was being prepared for burial to see how I would react. Maybe he thought that based on how I had reacted when they described the murder, the sight of the body would have an effect on me. The magistrate and several other people escorted me to the inn. I couldn't help but notice the strange coincidences that had happened on this eventful night. But since I knew I had been talking to a few people on the island around the time the body was found, I wasn't worried about what would happen next.

277   I went into the room where the body was placed and was led to the coffin. I can't even begin to describe how I felt when I saw it. It still gives me chills and makes me shudder to think about that terrible moment. The examination, the presence of the magistrate and witnesses, all fade from my memory when I saw Henry Clerval's lifeless body in front of me. I couldn't breathe, and I fell onto the body, saying, "Have my evil plans taken away your life too, my dearest Henry? I've already destroyed two; there are more victims waiting: but you, Clerval, my friend, my helper--"

I couldn't bear the agony any longer, and I was taken out of the room while having strong convulsions.

After that, I got a fever. I was on the brink of death for two months. I later learned that I had been saying horrible things in my delirium. I called myself the murderer of William, Justine, and Clerval. Sometimes I would beg the people taking care of me to help me destroy the monster who was tormenting me. Other times, I felt the monster's fingers squeezing my neck, and I would scream in pain and fear. Thankfully, only Mr. Kirwin understood me since I was speaking in my native language. But my wild gestures and cries scared the other witnesses.

278   Why didn't I die? I was more miserable than anyone has ever been before. Why didn't I just forget everything and find rest? Death takes away many young children, the only hope of their loving parents. How many brides and young lovers have gone from being healthy and hopeful one day to being food for worms and rotting in the grave the next! What am I made of that I can endure so much pain, like a never-ending torture?

But I was destined to live. After two months, I woke up from what felt like a dream, but I was actually in a prison. I was lying on a terrible bed, with guards, keys, locks, and all the awful things you find in a dungeon. It was morning when I woke up and started to understand what had happened. I couldn't remember all the details, but I felt like something terrible had happened to me. When I looked around and saw the barred windows and the filthy room I was in, the memories came flooding back, and I couldn't help but groan in despair.

279   This sound woke up an old woman who was sleeping in a chair next to me. She was a nurse that was hired to take care of me. Her face showed all the bad qualities that are often seen in people of her kind. Her face looked hard and rough, like someone who is used to seeing but not caring about miserable things. Her voice sounded familiar, like someone I had heard during my difficult times.

"Are you feeling better now, sir?" she asked me in English.

I weakly replied in the same language, "I think I am, but if everything is true, if I didn't just dream it all, then I'm sorry that I am still alive to feel this misery and horror."

"As for that," the old woman replied, "if you're talking about the man you killed, I think it would be better for you if you were dead. I think things are going to be very tough for you! But that's not my concern. I am here to take care of you and help you get well. I do my job with a clear conscience. It would be good if everyone did the same."

I turned away from the woman with disgust. How could she say such heartless things to someone who had just been saved from the brink of death? But I was too weak to think about everything that had happened. My whole life seemed like a dream to me. Sometimes I doubted if it had really happened, because it didn't feel real in my mind.

280   As I saw clearer images in my mind, I started feeling feverish. I was surrounded by darkness, with no one comforting me with love or supporting me with a caring hand. The doctor came and prescribed medicine, but the old woman who prepared it gave me a nasty look. No one cared about me.

These were my initial thoughts, but I soon discovered that Mr. Kirwin had shown me great kindness. He had arranged for the best room in the prison to be prepared for me, although even the best was miserable. He had also provided a doctor and a nurse. He didn't visit me often, as he didn't want to witness the suffering and hear the painful ramblings of a murderer. He only came occasionally to make sure I wasn't being neglected, but his visits were short and far between.

One day, as I was slowly getting better, I sat in a chair with my eyes half open and my pale cheeks resembling those of a person who is dead. I was filled with sadness and misery, and often thought it would be better for me to seek death than to want to stay in a world that seemed full of unhappiness. At one point, I even considered confessing my guilt and facing the punishment of the law, even though I was not as innocent as poor Justine who had suffered unjustly. Those were my thoughts when the door to my room opened and Mr. Kirwin came in. His face showed compassion and concern. He pulled a chair close to mine and spoke to me in French,

"I imagine this place must be very distressing for you. Is there anything I can do to make you more comfortable?"

"Thank you, but anything you could offer means nothing to me. There is no comfort in the world that I am capable of receiving."

"I understand that the sympathy of a stranger can only provide a small bit of relief for someone burdened with such a strange misfortune as you. But I hope that you will soon leave this sad place, as I believe there is proof that can clear you of the crime you are charged with."

"That is the least of my worries. Through a series of strange events, I have become the most miserable person alive. With all the persecution and torment I have endured, can death really be considered an evil to me?"

"Nothing could be more unfortunate and painful than the strange events that have happened recently. You were brought to this hospitable shore by a surprising accident, but then immediately seized and accused of murder. The first thing you saw was the body of your friend, murdered in a way that makes no sense, almost like it was deliberately placed in your path by some evil force."

As Mr. Kirwin spoke, I felt both the agitation caused by recalling my sufferings and surprise at his knowledge about me. My expression must have shown some astonishment because Mr. Kirwin quickly added,

"As soon as you fell ill, all the papers you had on you were given to me. I examined them in the hope of finding some clue that would allow me to inform your family about your misfortune and illness. I found several letters, including one from your father, which I recognized from its beginning. I immediately wrote to Geneva, but it has been almost two months since I sent the letter. But you're not well; you're trembling even now. You shouldn't be subjected to any more agitation."

"The suspense is a thousand times worse than the most horrible event. Please tell me what new tragedy has occurred and whose murder I am now mourning."

"Your family is perfectly fine," Mr. Kirwin said gently. "And a friend has come to visit you."

I don't know how it happened, but suddenly I had a thought. A terrible thought. I believed that the murderer had come to mock me and torment me with Clerval's death, as if it would make me do what he wanted. Overwhelmed with fear, I covered my eyes and cried out in pain,

"Oh! Get him away! I can't bear to see him. Please, don't let him come near me!"

Mr. Kirwin looked at me with concern. He interpreted my outburst as an admission of guilt and responded sternly,

"Young man, I would have expected your father's presence to bring joy, not such strong aversion."

"My father!" I exclaimed, my face and body instantly changing from agony to delight. "Has my father truly arrived? How kind, how incredibly kind! But where is he? Why isn't he rushing to see me?"

My sudden shift in demeanor surprised and pleased the magistrate. Perhaps he believed that my earlier outburst was just a fleeting moment of delirium. He quickly regained his kindness. He stood up, left the room with my nurse, and in no time, my father entered.

At that moment, the arrival of my father brought me immense joy. I reached out my hand to him and asked,

"Are you safe? And what about Elizabeth and Ernest?"

My dad comforted me, but he could see that being in prison made it hard to be happy. "This is not a good place for you to be, son," he said sadly, looking at the barred windows and the terrible condition of the room. "You went on a journey to find happiness, but it seems like bad luck keeps following you. And poor Clerval—"

Just hearing the name of my friend who was murdered was too much for me in my weak state; I started crying.

"Oh, yes, father," I replied, "there is some terrible fate hanging over me, and I have to live to fulfill it. Otherwise, I would have died when Henry did."

We weren't allowed to talk for very long because I was still recovering and needed to rest. Mr. Kirwin came in and told me to rest. But seeing my father was like having my guardian angel with me, and little by little, I started feeling better.

As I got better, a dark and sad feeling took control of me, and nothing could make it go away. The image of Clerval's gruesome murder haunted me all the time. My friends worried that these thoughts might make me sick again. Why did they save me from such a miserable and hated life? It must be because I have a destiny to fulfill, and it's almost over now. Death will come soon and stop these painful feelings, freeing me from the heavy burden of sorrow. When justice is served, I will finally find peace. Death seemed far away, but I wished for it often. I would sit quietly without saying a word for hours, hoping for a big change that would bury me and the one who caused all this suffering.

The time for the court hearings was coming near. I had already been in prison for three months. Even though I was still weak and at risk of getting sick again, I had to travel almost a hundred miles to the town where the court was held. Mr. Kirwin took care of gathering witnesses and preparing my defense. Thankfully, I didn't have to face the shame of being seen as a criminal, as my case was not brought before the court that decides whether someone lives or dies. The grand jury rejected the charges when it was proven that I was on the Orkney Islands when my friend's body was found. Two weeks after I was moved, I was set free from prison.

My father was overjoyed to see me released from the burden of being accused of a crime. He was glad that I could breathe the fresh air again and return home. But I couldn't share in his happiness. Both the walls of a dungeon and a palace were equally detestable to me. Life had become forever poisoned, and even though the sun shone upon me like it did for happy people, all around me I saw nothing but a thick and terrifying darkness. There was no light, except for the faint glimmer of two eyes staring at me. Sometimes, those eyes were the kind and loving eyes of Henry, now dead, with his dark orbs almost hidden beneath his eyelids and his long black lashes. And sometimes, those eyes were the watery, cloudy eyes of the monster, the first time I saw them in my room at Ingolstadt.

287   My father tried to make me feel affectionate. He talked about how I would soon go to Geneva and see Elizabeth and Ernest. But hearing these words made me let out deep groans. Sometimes, I did feel a desire for happiness. I would think sadly about my beloved cousin or yearn with a strong homesickness. Most of the time, I felt numb and indifferent, and I didn't care whether I was in a prison or in the most beautiful natural setting. These moments were rarely interrupted, except when I had sudden bursts of pain and despair. I was so deeply sad.

288   But I knew I had one more important responsibility left, even though I was consumed by my own sadness. I needed to go back to Geneva as soon as possible and protect the people I loved so much. I also needed to find the murderer and make sure they couldn't hurt

me or anyone else again. This monstrous creature, who I believed had a soul even more monstrous, needed to be stopped.

My father wanted to delay our journey because he worried that I wouldn't be able to handle the physical demands of traveling. And he was right - I was barely hanging on. I was like a fragile shadow, a mere skeleton of a person. I had lost all my strength. Day and night, I was plagued by fever, which further weakened my already deteriorating body.

289 But because I was so anxious and eager to leave Ireland, my father decided it was best to go. We got on a ship that was going to Havre-de-Grace and sailed away with a good wind. It was nighttime, and I was lying on the deck, looking up at the stars and listening to the sound of the waves crashing against the ship. I felt a sense of relief as I couldn't see Ireland anymore, and my heart raced with excitement knowing that I would soon be in Geneva. The past seemed like a terrible nightmare to me. But being on this ship, the wind blowing me away from Ireland, and the sea surrounding me reminded me that it was all real. My friend Clerval had become a victim of me and the monster I created. I thought back on my whole life – the peaceful times with my family in Geneva, the death of my mother, and when I left for Ingolstadt. I couldn't help but shudder as I remembered the intense excitement that drove me to create my hideous enemy, and I thought about the night he came to life. I couldn't continue my train of thought; countless emotions overwhelmed me, and I cried uncontrollably.

290 After I got better from the sickness, I started taking a little bit of medicine called laudanum every night. It was the only way I could get enough rest to stay alive. But because I was so haunted by all the bad things that happened to me, I took double my usual dose and fell into a deep sleep. Even though I was asleep, I still had scary dreams. When morning came, I felt like I was trapped in a nightmare. I felt someone holding onto my neck, and I couldn't break free. I heard groans and cries all around me. My father, who was watching over me, noticed that I was restless and woke me up. I saw the rough

waves and the cloudy sky above me. The terrifying creature wasn't there. I felt a little safer, like there was a break in the never-ending disaster that was waiting for me. It made me forget about all my worries for a short while, which is something the human mind is especially good at doing.

CHAPTER

TWENTY-TWO

291 OUR JOURNEY CAME TO AN END. We arrived in Paris. But I realized I needed to rest before continuing. My father took great care of me, trying to help with my suffering, but he didn't know why I was feeling this way. He thought going out and being social would make me feel better. But I couldn't stand being around people. Well, not exactly couldn't stand, because they were my fellow human beings and I actually felt drawn to them, even the ones who weren't pleasant. I saw them as angelic beings. But I felt like I didn't have the right to be with them. I had created an enemy among them, a creature that enjoyed hurting them and making them suffer. If they knew what I had done, they would all hate me and chase me away.

Eventually, my father gave in to my wish to avoid society. He tried to convince me that being accused of murder shouldn't make me feel so ashamed. He said pride was worthless.

292 "Oh no, my father," I said, feeling sad. "You don't understand me at all. If someone like me were to feel proud, it would degrade human beings and their emotions. Justine, poor Justine, was innocent just like me, but she was accused too. She died because of it, and it's my

135

fault—I killed her. William, Justine, and Henry—all of them died because of me."

During my time in prison, I often said the same thing to my father. Sometimes, he seemed curious and wanted me to explain, but other times he dismissed it as a product of my illness, thinking that during my recovery, I had imagined such things. I avoided giving an explanation and remained silent about the monster I had created. I was afraid that people would think I was crazy, and that alone kept me from speaking. But there was another reason—I couldn't bear to reveal a secret that would terrify and horrify my father. So, I suppressed my desperate need for understanding and chose silence, even though I longed to share the terrible truth. Yet, despite my efforts, words like the ones I just spoke would burst out of me uncontrollably. I couldn't explain them, but expressing them helped a little with the weight of my mysterious sorrow.

293   One day, my father looked at me with great surprise and said, "My dear Victor, why are you saying such unbelievable things? Please, my dear son, never make that claim again."

"No, I'm not crazy," I exclaimed passionately. "The sun and the heavens have witnessed my actions and can testify to the truth. I am responsible for the deaths of those innocent victims; they died because of what I did. I would have given my own life, drop by drop, to save them. But, Father, I couldn't sacrifice the entire human race."

After hearing this, my father believed that my thoughts were confused. He immediately changed the subject, trying to divert my attention and erase the memory of what happened in Ireland. He never mentioned those events again and didn't allow me to talk about the misfortunes I had faced.

As time went on, I became calmer. Misery lived in my heart, but I no longer spoke in that same disorganized manner about my own crimes. Knowing and acknowledging them myself was enough for me. I had to control the strong desire to reveal everything to the world. My behavior was more composed and peaceful than it had been since I traveled to the icy sea.

A few days before we left Paris to go to Switzerland, I received a letter from Elizabeth. It said:

"Dear Friend,

"I was overjoyed to receive a letter from my uncle in Paris. You are now closer, and I hope to see you in less than two weeks. I can only imagine how much you must have suffered. I expect you to look even worse than when you left Geneva. This winter has been terrible for me too, as I've been tortured by worry. However, I hope to see peace in your face and that you find some comfort and calmness in your heart.

Yet, I'm afraid that the same feelings that made you so miserable a year ago still exist, and maybe even worse with time. I don't want to trouble you during this difficult time when so many misfortunes burden you, but I had a conversation with my uncle before he left, and it requires some explanation before we meet.

You might wonder, why does Elizabeth need to explain anything? If you do wonder that, then all my questions are answered, and my doubts are relieved. However, since you are far away, it's possible that you both fear and desire this explanation. With that possibility in mind, I can no longer postpone writing what I've wanted to say to you during your absence, but never had the courage to start."

"Victor, you know that our parents always wanted us to get married. They told us this when we were young, and we were taught to expect it to happen someday. We were close friends when we were kids and as we got older, I think we became even dearer to each other. But sometimes, brothers and sisters can have a strong bond without wanting to be closer than that. Could that be true for us too? Please tell me, my dearest Victor. I beg you to answer honestly, for the sake of our happiness together—do you love someone else?"

You have traveled and spent many years in Ingolstadt. I must admit, my friend, that when I saw you so unhappy last autumn, isolating yourself from everyone, I started to think that maybe you no longer wanted to be in our relationship. I must confess, my friend, that I love you deeply, and in my dreams of the future, you have always been my loyal friend and companion. However, I want your happiness as much as my own. So, I want you to know that our marriage would make me forever unhappy unless it is your own choice, freely made. Oh, Victor, please know that I have genuine love for you, and I would be devastated if you thought otherwise. Please, be happy, my friend. And if you grant me this one request, know that nothing in this world could disturb my peace.

297   Please do not let this letter upset you. You don't have to reply tomorrow or the next day. I don't want to make you sad. My uncle will keep me updated. I only hope to see you smiling when you return. That would make me incredibly happy.

Elizabeth Lavenza.

Geneva, May 18th, 17—.

〰

READING this letter reminded me of something I had forgotten: the fiend's threat – "I will be with you on your wedding night!" That was my punishment. The monster promised to do everything to destroy me and take away the happiness that was starting to bring solace to my pain. He had planned to fulfill his wicked deeds by killing me. Well, so be it. A fierce fight would surely happen that night. If he won, I would finally find peace, and his control over me would end. If I defeated him, I would be a free man. But what kind of freedom? It would be like what a peasant experiences after witnessing the massacre of his family, his home burned, his land ruined, and being left homeless, poor, and alone, but free. That would be my version of freedom, except that I have Elizabeth, who is a precious treasure to me. Unfortunately, she is overshadowed by the burden of remorse and guilt that would haunt me until death.

298   Sweet and beloved Elizabeth! I read her letter over and over again, and it brought some gentle feelings into my heart. It made me dream of love and happiness, like paradise. But unfortunately, the

damage was already done, and I knew that my hope was being taken away. Still, I would do anything to make her happy. If the monster followed through on his threat, death was certain. However, I wondered if getting married would make my death come even sooner. Perhaps my tormentor would suspect that I was postponing it because of his threats, and he would find another, maybe even worse, way to get revenge. He had promised to be with me on my wedding night, but he didn't think that meant he had to leave me alone until then. In fact, he showed me that he still wanted more blood by killing Clerval right after making the threats. So, I decided that if marrying my cousin right away would bring happiness to her or our father, I wouldn't let my enemy's plans to end my life delay it for even a moment.

299   I sent a letter to Elizabeth in the state of mind I was in. My letter was calm and loving. "My dear girl," I wrote, "I'm afraid there is not much happiness left for us in this world. But everything I hope to enjoy one day revolves around you. Please don't let your fears get the best of you. I dedicate my life to you and will do everything I can to make us happy. There's one secret, Elizabeth, a dreadful one. It's so terrible that when I tell you, it will fill you with horror. You won't be surprised by my unhappiness, but rather wonder how I managed to survive what I've been through. I promise to tell you about this tale of misery and terror the day after our wedding. My dear cousin, we must have complete trust in each other. But until then, I beg you not to bring it up or mention it. I desperately ask this of you, and I believe you will agree."

About a week later, we returned to Geneva after receiving Elizabeth's letter. The sweet girl greeted me with warm affection, but there were tears in her eyes when she saw how thin and sickly I looked. I noticed a change in her too. She had lost weight and didn't have the same lively spirit that had charmed me before. But her kindness and compassionate gaze made her an even better companion for someone like me, who was broken and miserable.

300   The peace that I felt didn't last. Remembering what had

happened made me lose my mind. Sometimes I was angry and filled with rage. Sometimes I felt sad and hopeless. I didn't speak to anyone or even look at them. I just sat still, feeling overwhelmed by all the misery that engulfed me.

Only Elizabeth had the power to bring me out of these episodes. Her gentle voice would calm me when I was filled with strong emotions and remind me to feel like a human when I felt numb. She cried with me and for me. When I regained my sanity, she would talk to me and try to encourage me to accept my situation. It's good for the unfortunate to accept their fate, but for the guilty, there is no peace. The pain of regret ruins any comfort that comes from indulging in excessive grief.

Not long after I arrived, my father mentioned my upcoming marriage to Elizabeth. I didn't say anything.

"Do you have feelings for someone else?" he asked.

"No one on this earth. I love Elizabeth and I am excited for us to be together. Let's set a date for our wedding, and on that day, I will devote myself completely to her happiness, even if it means sacrificing my own life."

"Dear Victor, please don't talk like that. We've had some really bad things happen, but let's hold onto what's left and shift our love from those we've lost to those who are still here. Our group will be small, but we'll be close because of our affection and shared misfortune. And when time lessens your sadness, new and dear things to care for will come along to replace the ones we've lost so cruelly."

That's what my father told me. But I couldn't forget the threat: it made sense to think that the fiend, all-powerful in his violent actions, would be impossible to defeat. When he said, "I will be with you on your wedding night," I saw that destiny as something unavoidable. But death wasn't scary to me if it meant I wouldn't lose Elizabeth. So, I agreed with my father, looking content and even happy, that if my cousin agreed, we would have the ceremony in ten days. I thought this would seal my destiny.

My goodness! If I had only known what evil plans my monstrous enemy had in mind! I would have rather left my homeland and wandered the world alone, without any friends, than agree to this terrible marriage. But somehow, the monster had tricked me and I couldn't see his true intentions. I thought I was only preparing for my own death, but in reality, I was hastening the death of someone much dearer to me.

As the day of our wedding got closer, I started feeling my heart sink. I tried not to make my sadness obvious, but Elizabeth, with her ever-watchful eyes, could see through my act. She looked forward to our marriage with a calm happiness, although there was a little bit of fear mixed in. The hardships we had faced in the past had left her with the belief that what seemed like certain and tangible happiness now might fade away like a daydream, leaving only deep and ever-lasting regret.

303 Preparations were made for the big event. People came over to congratulate us, and everyone seemed happy. My father had managed to get part of Elizabeth's inheritance back from the Austrian government. She owned a small piece of land by Lake Como. We agreed that after we got married, we would go to Villa Lavenza and spend our first happy days together by the beautiful lake.

In the meantime, I took precautions to protect myself in case the fiend decided to attack me openly. I carried guns and a knife with me at all times and stayed alert to avoid any tricks. This made me feel more calm and peaceful. I eventually grew comfortable and wasn't as worried about what might happen. Everyone talked about our wedding as an event that nothing could possibly stop.

304 Elizabeth appeared happy, and my calm demeanor helped put her at ease. However, on the day that was meant to fulfill my wishes and change my destiny, she seemed sad and had a feeling that something bad was going to happen. Perhaps she was also thinking about the terrible secret I had promised to tell her the next day. Meanwhile, my father was overjoyed and in the excitement of the preparations, he only saw Elizabeth's sadness as the nervousness of a bride.

After the wedding ceremony, a big group of people gathered at my father's house. We had decided that Elizabeth and I would start our journey by boat, spending the night in Evian and continuing the next day. The weather was nice, the wind was favorable, and everything seemed perfect for our wedding boat trip.

Those were the last moments of my life when I felt truly happy. We sailed quickly along the lake, staying protected from the hot sun under a canopy. We saw stunning shores and mountains.

305   I held Elizabeth's hand and said, "You seem sad, my love. If only you knew the pain I have endured and may still face. Please, let me enjoy this one day of peace and hope."

"Don't worry, Victor," Elizabeth replied. "There's nothing to trouble you. Even though I may not look ecstatic, my heart is content. Something tells me not to get too carried away with our future, but I won't listen to those negative thoughts. Look how fast we're moving, and how the clouds above Mont Blanc add to the beauty of this scene. And see all the fish swimming in the clear water, every pebble visible at the bottom. What a perfect day! Nature is so happy and peaceful."

Elizabeth tried to distract herself, as well as me, from any melancholy thoughts. But her mood kept changing. Happiness would briefly light up her eyes, only to be replaced by distraction and daydreaming.

306   The sun moved lower in the sky. We crossed the Drance River and saw how it flowed through the narrow spaces between the tall hills. The Alps came closer to the lake here, and we got closer to the mountains. We could see the top of Evian peeking out from the woods that surrounded it.

The strong wind that had been pushing us along suddenly died down at sunset, leaving only a gentle breeze. The soft air caused a pleasant movement among the trees as we neared the shore. From there, we could smell the wonderful scents of flowers and freshly cut hay. The sun disappeared below the horizon just as we reached the land. And as I stepped onto the shore, I felt the worries and fears that would soon consume me come alive once again, never to let go.

CHAPTER
TWENTY-THREE

 IT WAS eight o'clock when we arrived. We took a short walk along the shore. After that, we went back to the inn and enjoyed more pleasant views.

The wind, which had calmed down from the south, suddenly picked up again, this time blowing fiercely from the west. The moon had reached its highest point in the sky and was starting to descend. There were many birds in the air. They looked like vultures. Suddenly, a heavy rainstorm began.

I had been calm during the day, but as soon as night arrived and objects became less visible, a thousand fears filled my mind. I was anxious and alert, with a pistol hidden in my pocket. Every sound scared me, but I made a decision that I would fight fiercely, not backing down until either my opponent or I were defeated.

Elizabeth watched my restlessness in silence, feeling scared and uneasy. She could tell from my expression that something was wrong and asked me nervously, "What is bothering you, my dear Victor? What are you afraid of?"

"Oh, please, my love," I replied, "everything will be alright tonight. But this night is dreadful, very dreadful."

308   I spent an hour in this worried state, then I realized how scary it would be for my wife if the fight I was expecting happened. I begged her to leave and promised to join her later, once I knew where my enemy was.

She left, and I walked through the house for a while, searching every corner where my adversary could be hiding. But I found no trace of him, and started thinking that maybe something lucky prevented him from carrying out his threats. Suddenly, I heard a loud and terrifying scream. It came from the room where Elizabeth had gone. When I heard it, I instantly understood what had happened. My arms went limp, I couldn't move a muscle. I felt my blood running cold through my veins, and my limbs started tingling. This state only lasted a moment; then I heard the scream again, and I burst into the room.

309   Oh no! Why didn't I die then! Why am I still here to tell the tragic tale of the destruction of the most hopeful and pure being on Earth? She lay lifeless and motionless on the bed, her head drooping, her pale and twisted face partially hidden by her hair. The sight was a shock and I didn't even know if I could go on living. For a brief moment, I lost consciousness and collapsed onto the ground.

When I regained consciousness, I found myself surrounded by the people from the inn. Their faces showed overwhelming terror, but their horror seemed insignificant compared to the weight of grief that engulfed me. I managed to escape from them and retreated to the room where Elizabeth's lifeless body lay. She was my love, my wife, who was so recently alive and so dear to me. She had been repositioned since I had last seen her. Her head was now resting on her arm, with a handkerchief placed delicately over her face and neck. At first glance, one might have thought she was asleep. I rushed towards her and embraced her tightly, but the lifelessness was clear. There was a dreadful mark on her neck from someone's grip.

310   As I hovered over her, feeling completely overwhelmed with despair, I glanced upwards. The room had been in darkness before,

so I was startled when I saw the pale light of the moon flooding the chamber. The shutters had been opened, and to my horror, I saw a figure standing at the open window. A wicked grin spread across the monster's face as he pointed towards my wife's lifeless body. I sprinted toward the window to grab at him, but he disappeared into the lake with unbelievable speed.

The sound of the gunshot drew a crowd into the room. I motioned towards where the monster had vanished, and we set out in boats to search for him. We cast nets into the water, but our efforts were in vain. After spending many hours in our search, we returned to shore filled with hopelessness. Most of my companions believed that what I had seen was a product of my imagination. Once we had disembarked, they split into groups and scoured the surrounding area, exploring various paths through the woods and vineyards.

311 I tried to go with them, walking a short way from the house. But my head felt dizzy, and I stumbled around like a drunk person. Finally, I collapsed from exhaustion. My vision became blurry, and my skin was dry from fever. They brought me back to the house and laid me on a bed. I barely knew what had happened. I looked around the room, searching for something I had lost.

After some time, I got up and, as if on instinct, crawled into the room where my beloved's body lay. There were women crying all around. I leaned over the body, joining them in shedding tears. During that time, my mind couldn't form clear thoughts. My thinking wandered, mixing up my misfortunes and their causes. I was lost in confusion and terrified. The death of William, the punishment of Justine, the murder of Clerval, and finally, my wife's death - even at that moment, I didn't know if my remaining friends were safe from the monster's evil plans. My father could be suffering under his grip right now, and Ernest could be dead. The thought made me tremble, bringing me back to my senses. I jumped up and decided to quickly return to Geneva.

312 There were no horses available, so I had to go back by the lake. The wind was against me, and it was raining heavily. However, it

was still early in the day, and I thought I could make it back by night-time. I hired some men to row the boat, and I took an oar myself. I always found relief from my troubled mind through physical activity. But this time, I was overwhelmed by sadness and couldn't find the strength to row. I dropped the oar and rested my head in my hands, allowing all the gloomy thoughts to take over. When I looked up, I saw familiar scenes from happier times, the ones I had seen just the day before with the person who is now only a memory. Tears streamed down my face. I could not believe the quick change in my life. I was happy just earlier and now I was hopeless. A fiend had taken away all hope of future happiness from me. I had never been so miserable, and such a horrifying event is unique in human history.

313   But why should I keep talking about what happened after that terrible event? My story has been full of horrifying things. It has reached its worst point, and what I have to tell you now might just be boring. Just know that, one by one, my friends were taken away from me, leaving me alone. I am completely worn out and must now summarize the rest of my terrible story in just a few words.

I finally arrived in Geneva. My father and Ernest were still alive, but my father couldn't bear the news I brought. His eyes had lost their sparkle and joy, and they just wandered aimlessly. Elizabeth, who he loved like a daughter, brought him so much happiness. He cherished her deeply, especially at this stage of his life when he didn't have many loved ones left. I curse the monster who brought such misery to my father's old age. His will to live suddenly disappeared. He couldn't even get out of bed, and in just a few days, he passed away in my arms.

314   What happened to me after that? I don't know. I lost all feeling and was surrounded by chains and darkness. I felt so sad, but over time, I started to understand my terrible circumstances and the misery I was in. Eventually, they let me out of my prison because they believed I was insane. It turned out that for many months, I had been locked away in a small, lonely cell.

But freedom didn't mean much to me unless I also awakened to seek revenge as I regained my sanity. As I remembered the terrible things that had happened to me, I started to think about why it all happened. All of this was because of the monster that I had created, the wretched creature that I had unleashed into the world to destroy me. Whenever I thought of him, I filled with an uncontrollable rage. I wanted and needed revenge.

My hatred didn't stay limited to just wishing for revenge. I started to think about how I could capture him. About a month after being released, I went to a judge in town and told him I had an accusation to make. I said that I knew the murderer who destroyed my family and asked him to use his power to arrest this monster.

315   The judge listened to me carefully and kindly. "Rest assured, sir," he said, "I will spare no effort to uncover the culprit."

"Thank you," I replied. "Please, then, listen to my statement. It is a tale so strange that I fear you might not believe it, but there is something true about it that, no matter how extraordinary, compels belief. The story is too coherent to be mistaken for a dream, and I have no reason to lie." I spoke in a calm manner. In my heart, I had resolved to pursue my destroyer to the end, and this purpose calmed my pain and, for a time, made me accept life. Briefly, but confidently and precisely, I recounted my history, noting the dates accurately and avoiding angry outbursts or exclamations.

At first, the judge seemed skeptical, but as I continued, he became more attentive and interested. Sometimes, I noticed him shudder with horror.

When I finished my story, I said, "This is the person I accuse, and I urge you to use all your power to catch and punish them. It is your duty as a judge, and I believe and hope that your compassion as a human being will not prevent you from carrying out your responsibilities on this matter."

316   As I spoke, I saw a change in the face of the person listening to me. He had heard my story, but only half believed it, thinking it was just a tale about ghosts and strange happenings. But now, when he had to take official action, his doubts returned. Still, he replied

gently, "I want to help you in your search, but the creature you describe seems to have powers that would make it impossible for me to catch. How can you follow something that can cross icy seas and hide in dangerous, forbidden places? Also, it's been many months since he committed his crimes, so who knows where he may be now."

"I believe he's close to where I live, and if he's hiding in the Alps, we can hunt him down like we would a wild animal. We can destroy him as a dangerous predator. But I can tell what you're thinking—you don't believe what I'm saying, and you don't plan to punish my enemy like they deserve."

As I spoke, my anger showed in my eyes, and the magistrate became intimidated. He said, "You are mistaken. I will do my best to capture the monster, and he will face punishment for his crimes. However, based on what you have described about the creature, it may not be possible to catch him. While we take the necessary steps, be prepared for the possibility of disappointment."

"That's not acceptable. But I understand that my need for revenge doesn't matter to you. Yet, I admit that it is the over-whelming passion in my life. I am filled with unspeakable rage knowing that the murderer I set loose is still out there. Since you cannot help me, I have only one option left. I will dedicate myself, either in life or death, to destroying him."

As I spoke these words, I was shaking. To a magistrate from Geneva, who was focused on different matters, my mindset appeared to be madness. He tried to calm me down like a nurse would soothe a child, believing my words were delirious.

"Man," I cried out, "your pride blinds you to your ignorance! Stop! You don't understand what you're saying."

I left the house feeling angry and upset. I went somewhere quiet to think about what else I could do.

TWENTY-FOUR

319 I WAS SO CAUGHT up in my current situation that I couldn't think clearly. Anger consumed me, but it also gave me strength to stay focused. Instead of losing control, I became calculating and composed. I knew I had to leave Geneva behind forever. Even though it used to be dear to me when life was good, now it felt unbearable. I gathered some money and jewelry that belonged to my mother and set off on a journey.

And so, my travels began, which won't end until I die. I've been to many places on this earth and endured countless hardships that travelers face in deserts and uncivilized lands. I don't even know how I managed to survive. Many times, I prayed for death as I lay exhausted in the sand. But revenge kept me going. I couldn't die and let my enemy continue to live.

320 When I left Geneva, my first task was to find a clue that would help me track down my evil enemy. However, I didn't have a clear plan, so I wandered around the outskirts of the town for many hours, unsure of which path to take. As it got dark, I found myself at the entrance of the cemetery where William, Elizabeth, and my father were laid to rest. It felt like the spirits of the departed were hovering

around, casting a shadow over me. I could feel it, although I could not see it.

321   I was overwhelmed with sorrow when I saw this heartbreaking scene, but soon that sorrow turned into anger and hopelessness. They were gone, and I was left alive. The person who killed them was still alive too, and in order to get rid of my misery, I had to continue living. I knelt down on the grass and kissed the ground. With trembling lips, I said, "I swear by this sacred earth I'm kneeling on, by the spirits that are near me, and by the deep and everlasting sadness I feel, I will pursue the monster who caused this pain until either he or I am defeated. I will keep myself alive for this purpose. I will see the sun again and walk on the green grass of the earth. I ask you, spirits of the dead, let that cursed and wicked creature suffer greatly. Let him feel the despair that I am feeling right now."

I started my plea in a serious and solemn manner, feeling like the spirits of my murdered friends were listening and approving. But as I finished, anger took over me and I couldn't speak anymore.

322   In the quiet of the night, a wicked and loud laugh pierced the silence. It echoed through the mountains. The laughter faded away, and then a voice I recognized, one that I despised, whispered in my ear, "I am pleased. You pitiful creature! You've chosen to live, and I am pleased."

I rushed towards the source of the sound, but the devil slipped away from my grasp. Then, the full moon rose and illuminated his horrifying and twisted figure as he fled with incredible speed.

I chased after him for many months. By a strange stroke of luck, I saw the demon sneak onto a ship heading to the Black Sea at night. I managed to get on the same ship, but somehow, he escaped, and I don't know how.

323   Amidst the remote lands of Tartary and Russia, even though he managed to avoid me, I have always followed his trail. Sometimes, frightened peasants tell me they had seen him. Occasionally, he himself would leave some clue behind, fearing that if I lost all trace of him, I would lose hope and die. Cold, hunger, and exhaustion were

the least of the pains I was fated to endure. I was cursed by a devil. When I despaired the most, this spirit would rescue me from seemingly huge obstacles. Sometimes, when I was weakened by hunger and nature had abandoned me, a meal would miraculously appear. Throughout my journey, I'd find small gifts of relief here and there. It was like fate was helping my chase.

324   I followed the paths of rivers when I could, but the creature I was chasing usually stayed away from these areas because that's where most people lived. In other areas, I rarely saw any humans, so I relied on the wild animals I encountered for food. I had some money, which I used to make friends with the villagers by giving it to them. Sometimes, I brought food that I had hunted and shared a portion with those who had given me fire and cooking tools.

325   My life was miserable, except for when I was asleep. Sleep brought me joy and happiness in my dreams. It was like the spirits watching over me gave me these moments of happiness so I could stay strong on my journey. Without these moments of rest, I would have given up. During the day, I held on to the hope of night. In my dreams, I saw my friends, my wife, and my beloved country. I saw my father's kind face, heard my wife's lovely voice, and saw Clerval healthy and young. Sometimes, when I was tired from walking, I convinced myself that I was dreaming and that I would wake up with my dear friends by my side. I loved them so much and clung to the memories of them, even while I was awake. In those moments, my desire for revenge against the creature vanished, and I continued on my journey, not because I wanted to, but because it felt like I was being guided by some unseen force.

326   I do not know what the person I was chasing felt. Sometimes, though, he would leave messages on trees or stone that led me and made me angry. In one of these messages, it said, "I am still in control. You are alive, and I have all the power. Follow me. I am going to the icy north, where you will feel the freezing cold that I don't mind. If you follow quickly, you will find a dead hare near this place. Eat it and get refreshed. Keep coming, my enemy. We still have to

fight for our lives, but you will suffer many hard and miserable hours until that time comes."

Terrible devil! I will seek revenge once again. I will make you, miserable monster, suffer and die. I will never stop looking for you until one of us is gone. Then, I will finally join my Elizabeth and my friends who have passed away. They are waiting for me and will reward me for all the hard work and dreadful journey!

As I continued to travel north, the snow got thicker and it became extremely cold. It was almost too much to handle. The local people stayed inside their small houses, and only a few brave ones went out to catch animals that were desperate for food. The rivers were frozen, so I couldn't catch any fish, which was my main source of food.

327   The more difficult my tasks became, the more my enemy reveled in his triumph. One message he left said: "Get ready! Your hardships are just beginning. Wrap yourself in warm fur and gather food, because we will soon embark on a journey where your suffering will satisfy my hatred."

These mocking words only fueled my courage and determination. I made a firm decision not to give up on my mission. I continued on despite difficult and unfamiliar conditions. I did not weep, but instead knelt down and, with a heart full of gratitude, thanking the spirit for leading me safely to this place. Despite my adversary's mocking, it was here that I hoped to finally confront and wrestle with him.

328   A few weeks earlier, I had obtained a sled and some dogs, which allowed me to travel swiftly through the snowy terrain. I don't know if the creature had the same advantages, but I noticed that I was gaining on him. By the time I saw the ocean, he was only one day's journey ahead of me. I hoped to catch up to him before he reached the beach.

Feeling newfound courage, I continued onwards. In just two days, I arrived at a small and miserable village by the sea. I asked the villagers about the creature and they gave me detailed information.

They described a monstrous figure who had arrived the night before. He was armed with a gun and many pistols. He had also taken their winter food supply and loaded it onto a sled. To navigate the sled, he had forcibly taken control of a large group of trained dogs.

Under the horrified gaze of the villagers, he harnessed the dogs to the sled and continued his journey across the sea in a direction that led to no land. The villagers believed that he would soon die either by the breaking of the ice or the extreme cold.

329   Upon hearing this information, I felt momentarily overwhelmed with despair. The fiend had managed to escape me, and now I had to embark on a treacherous and seemingly never-ending journey across the frozen ocean. As someone from a warm place, I knew my own chances of survival were slim. However, I knew I needed to continue working towards my goals and seeking vengeance. I prepared myself for the journey ahead.

I traded in my land sled for one specifically designed for navigating the uneven surfaces of the Frozen Ocean. I also stocked up on plenty of food supplies before setting off from land.

I cannot say for certain how many days have passed since then. Time and time again, the freezing temperatures returned, establishing safe paths across the icy sea.

330   According to the amount of food I had eaten, I think I had been on this journey for about three weeks. The constant stretching of my hope only made me feel more and more hopeless and sad. Despair almost had me completely, and I was on the verge of giving up under this misery. Once, after the tired animals that were carrying me had finally reached the top of a slanted ice mountain, one of them became too exhausted and died. When I looked out at the vast icy plain before me, I felt a deep sadness. But then, something caught my eye—a dark spot on the dark plain. I focused my vision to see what it could be, and I couldn't believe it when I realized it was a sledge and the distorted shape of someone I knew. Oh! The feeling of hope flooded my heart with warmth! Tears filled my eyes, but I quickly wiped them away so I could see the creature clearly.

However, my sight was still blurry from the tears, and eventually, I couldn't hold back anymore and cried loudly.

331   But this was not the right time to wait. I removed the dead dog from the others, gave them plenty of food, and after resting for an hour, which was necessary but annoying for me, I continued on my journey. I could still see the sled, and I never lost sight of it again, except for when it was temporarily hidden by ice formations. I was actually getting closer to it, and when, after almost two days of traveling, I saw my enemy only a mile away. My heart leapt with excitement.

But just when I was so close to catching my enemy, my hopes were suddenly crushed, and I completely lost track of him even more than before. I heard the ground shaking beneath me, as the roar of the advancing sea grew more and more frightening. I tried to keep going, but it was useless. The wind picked up, the sea raged, and with a massive, earth-shaking explosion, it split and cracked apart. The process was quick. In a matter of minutes, a wild sea stood between me and my enemy, and I was left stranded on a shrinking piece of ice. I feared for my death.

332   In this way, I endured many terrifying hours. Some of my dogs died. I was on the verge of collapsing from the overwhelming distress. But then, I spotted your ship. Despite how I tired I was, I pushed my ice-raft towards your ship. Even if you were sailing south, I had decided to rely on the mercy of the seas rather than give up on my mission. My plan was to convince you to give me a boat so that I could continue chasing my enemy. However, you were heading north. When I was at my weakest point, you took me on board, saving me. But now, my mission remains unfinished.

333   Oh! When will my guiding spirit show me mercy and let me rest? Or must I die while he continues to live? If I do, promise me, Walton, that he won't escape. Promise me that you will find him and seek vengeance by ending his life. But should I really ask you to undertake my journey and endure the hardships I've faced? No, I am not that selfish. However, when I am no longer alive, if he should come to

you, if the bringers of vengeance should lead him to you, swear that he won't survive—swear that he won't triumph over my endless sorrows and continue his dark crimes. He is skilled at speaking and convincing, and his words once had an effect on my heart. But don't trust him. His soul is as wicked as his appearance, filled with deceit and evil intent. Don't listen to him. Instead, call upon the spirits of William, Justine, Clerval, Elizabeth, my father, and the miserable Victor. Thrust your sword into his heart. I will be close by, guiding your hand.

Walton, continuing his story.

August 26th, 17—.

334 Margaret, you have read this strange and terrifying story. Does it not make your blood run cold with horror, just like it does for me? Listening to him speak shows his range of emotions. He was sad, calm, but also so in need of revenge.

His story is logical and told with a sense of truth. Yet, I must admit, the letters from Felix and Safie that he showed me, and the sighting of the monster from our ship, convinced me even more. So, this monster truly exists! I cannot doubt it. I am simply astonished and amazed. At times, I tried to learn from Frankenstein how he created this creature, but he refused to share any details on this subject.

335 "Are you crazy, my friend?" he said. "Where does your senseless curiosity take you? Do you want to create a demonic enemy for yourself and the world? Calm down, calm down! Listen to my sorrows and don't try to make your own worse."

Frankenstein found out that I wrote down his story: he wanted to read it and made some changes and additions, especially when it came to the conversations he had with his enemy. "Now that you have recorded my story," he said, "I don't want a incomplete version to be passed on to future generations."

336   A week has passed and while I have listened to the strangest tale that ever imagination formed. My thoughts, and every feeling of my soul have been consumed by the interest for my guest. I want to comfort him, but he seems to only find comfort in his solitude and confusion. In other words, he believes that when he dreams about talking to his friends and finds comfort or motivation for his vengeance, they are not just creations of his imagination, but actual beings from another world. It is fascinating.

    Our conversations aren't always about his own story and hardships. He has an extensive knowledge of various subjects and a quick understanding. He speaks with force and emotion, and I can't help but cry when he tells a sad story or tries to evoke pity or love. What an amazing person he must have been when he was successful! Even in his downfall, he remains noble and remarkable. It seems like he understands his own value and the scale of his tragic fall.

337   "When I was younger," he began, "I believed that I was meant for something great. I thought it was wrong to waste my talents in useless sorrow when I could use them to help others. When I considered the work I had completed, I didn't see myself as just another ordinary dreamer. However, now this very thought that once lifted me up only drags me down further into despair. All my plans and hopes have amounted to nothing. From a young age, I was filled with lofty ambitions and great aspirations. But oh, how far I have fallen! My friend, if you had known me in my prime, you wouldn't believe this is the same person you see now, stripped of all glory. Despair rarely invaded my heart. It felt like a higher destiny was propelling me forward, until I fell and could never rise again."

338   Do I have to lose this amazing person? I've wanted a friend for so long, someone who understands and cares for me. And now, here, in the middle of nowhere, I've found that person. But I'm afraid I've only found him to realize how wonderful he is and then lose him. I want to help him see the good in life, but he pushes away that idea.

339   "Thank you, Walton," he said, "for being kind to someone as miserable as me. But when you talk about new connections and fresh

feelings, do you think anyone can replace the ones who are gone? Can anyone be to me what Clerval was, or can any woman be another Elizabeth? Even if the feelings aren't incredibly strong, the friends we had in childhood always have a certain hold on our minds that hardly any later friend can have. They know how we were when we were little, and even if we change as we grow up, those parts of us never completely go away. They can understand our actions and determine if our intentions are good. A sister or a brother could never suspect the other of being dishonest, unless there were early signs, but another friend, no matter how close, might sometimes be seen with suspicion. But I had friends who were special not just because we were used to each other's company, but because of their own qualities. And no matter where I am, I'll always hear the comforting voice of Elizabeth and the conversations with Clerval in my ear. They're gone now, and in such loneliness, there's only one reason for me to want to keep living. If I were involved in a big and important project that would help others, then I could live to complete it. But that's not what's meant for me. I have to pursue and kill the creature I made, and only then will my purpose on earth be fulfilled, and I can die."

340   September 2nd.

Dear Sister,

I am writing to you in a dangerous situation, unsure if I will ever see England again or the friends who mean so much to me. I am surrounded by huge icy mountains that trap us and could crush our ship at any moment. The brave men who agreed to accompany me are looking to me for help, but I have nothing to offer. Our situation is very frightening, but I still have courage and hope. It's hard to think that all of these men's lives are in danger because of me. If we perish, it will be because of my foolish plans.

And what will you be thinking, Margaret? I hope you never have to hear about my death and that you will eagerly wait for my return. Years will go by, and you will feel despair but still hold onto hope. Oh, my dear sister, the thought of you being disappointed and losing hope is more painful to me than my own death. But you have a husband and wonderful children, so you can be happy. May Heaven bless you and bring you happiness!

My guest, who is also unfortunate like me, looks at me with great kindness. He tries to give me hope and talks as if life is something valuable. He tells me stories of other sailors who faced similar accidents in this sea and still made it through. Despite myself, he fills me with positive thoughts. Even the sailors are inspired by his words. When he speaks, they stop feeling hopeless. He motivates them. However, these feelings don't last long. Every day we wait in uncertainty, fear starts creeping in, and I'm afraid there might be a mutiny caused by despair.

September 5th.

Something really interesting just happened, and even though it's very likely that you won't get to read about it, I can't help but write it down.

We're still surrounded by towering mountains of ice, and there's still a big risk of our ship being crushed. It's extremely cold, and many of my poor friends have. His eyes still show signs of fever, but he's exhausted. When he tries to do anything, he quickly becomes weak and lifeless again.

In my last letter, I told you about my concerns of a possible mutiny. This morning, something unexpected happened. I was sitting with my friend, who looked very weak and tired, when a group of sailors came to my cabin. They had been chosen to talk to me on behalf of the other sailors. They were worried that if we were freed from the ice and had a chance to escape, I might continue our risky journey instead of heading south to safety. They wanted me to promise that if we were freed, I would immediately change our course towards the south.

This request troubled me. I hadn't given up hope, and I hadn't thought about turning back if we were freed. But could I really refuse their demand? I couldn't decide right away. Just as I was hesitating,

Frankenstein, who had been quiet and weak, suddenly spoke up. He looked determined and energetic. Turning to the sailors, he said-

343   "What do you mean? What do you want from your captain? Are you so easily changing your plans? Didn't you call this expedition glorious? And why was it glorious? Not because the journey was easy and calm like a warm sea, but because it was filled with dangers and terror. Every new challenge required your strength and courage. You had to face danger and death and overcome them. That's what made it glorious, that's what made it an honorable mission. You were supposed to be praised as heroes, men who faced death for honor and the good of humanity. But now, at the first sign of danger, or if you prefer, the first huge test of your bravery, you shrink back and are satisfied being known as men who couldn't handle the cold and danger. So, poor souls, you felt a chill and returned to your warm firesides. Well, that doesn't require all this build-up. You didn't have to come this far and bring your captain to the shame of defeat just to prove you're cowards. Oh, be men, or even better than men. Stay true to your goals and be as strong as a rock. This ice isn't as strong as your hearts. It can change, and it won't withstand you if you decide it won't. Don't go back to your families with the shame of failure on your faces. Return as heroes who fought and conquered, who never turned their backs on the enemy."

344   With a voice that expressed different emotions throughout his speech and eyes filled with grand plans and bravery, he spoke. Can you understand why these men were moved? They looked at each other and couldn't respond. I spoke up and told them to go back and think about what had been said. I said that I wouldn't lead them further north if they strongly disagreed, but I hoped that with some time to think, their courage would return.

They went away, and I turned to my friend, but he was weak and close to death.

I don't know how this will end, but I would rather die than go back shamefully without completing my mission. Though I fear that will be my fate. The men, without the idea of glory and honor to support them, can't bear their hardships any longer.

September 7th.

It's decided; I have agreed to go back, if we don't get destroyed. My hopes have been ruined by cowardice and indecision. I'm returning ignorant and disappointed. I need more strength than I have to handle this injustice with patience.

September 12th.

It's done; I'm going back to England. I've lost my dreams of helping others and gaining glory. I've lost my friend. But I will try to explain all these painful details to you, my dear sister. As I sail towards England and towards you, I won't lose hope.

345 September 9th, the ice started to move, and there were loud rumblings like thunder as the islands cracked in every direction. We were in great danger, but since we could do nothing about it, I focused on my unfortunate guest, whose sickness got worse and he had to stay in bed. The ice cracked behind us and was pushed forcefully towards the north. A breeze came from the west, and on the 11th, the path to the south became completely clear. When the sailors saw this and realized they were going back home, they shouted with joyful excitement for a long time. Frankenstein woke up from his nap and asked why they were making so much noise. "They're shouting," I said, "because they'll soon return to England."

"Do you really plan to go back too?"

"Sadly, yes. I can't refuse their request. I can't lead them into danger against their will, so I have to go back."

"If that's what you want, go ahead. But I won't. I can't give up on my purpose. Heaven has given it to me, and I can't ignore it. I may be weak, but I believe the spirits helping me seek revenge will give me enough strength." He tried to get out of bed, but it was too much for him. He fell back and passed out.

346 It took a while before he got better, and I thought he was dead. Finally, he opened his eyes, but he couldn't breathe or talk easily. The doctor gave him some medicine to help him calm down and told us

to leave him alone. The doctor also said that my friend didn't have much time left to live.

347   His punishment was given, and I could only be sad and patient. I sat by his bed, watching him. His eyes were closed, and I thought he was sleeping. But then, he called me in a weak voice and asked me to come closer. He said, "Oh no! The strength I relied on is gone. I feel like I'm going to die soon, and my enemy, the one who tormented me, might still be alive. Please don't think, Walton, that in my last moments I feel that burning hatred and intense desire for revenge that I once had. But I do feel that it's justified to wish for the death of my enemy. These last days, I've been thinking about my past actions, and I don't find them blameworthy. In a moment of crazed enthusiasm, I created a thinking being and took on the responsibility of ensuring his happiness and well-being as much as I could. That was my duty, but there was another duty that was even more important. My duties towards other human beings had stronger claims on my attention because they could experience more happiness or misery. With that in mind, I refused to create a companion for the first creature. He showed unmatched evil and selfishness. He destroyed my friends and sentenced to death beings who had the ability to feel joy, happiness, and wisdom. And I have no idea where this thirst for revenge will end. He should die so that he doesn't make anyone else miserable. It was my job to destroy him, but I have failed. When I was driven by selfish and wicked motives, I asked you to continue my unfinished work. And now, when I'm guided by reason and virtue, I ask you again."

348   "But I can't ask you to leave your country and friends behind to complete this task. And now that you're going back to England, it's unlikely that you'll have a chance to find him. But I'll leave it up to you to consider these things and weigh what you believe to be your responsibilities. My thoughts and judgment are already clouded by the impending approach of death. I can't bring myself to ask you to do what I think is right because I might still be influenced by my emotions.

The fact that he could continue causing harm troubles me. Good-bye, Walton! Find happiness in peace and avoid ambition, even if its to distinguish yourself in science and discoveries. Then again, why am I saying this? My own hopes in these pursuits have been destroyed, but someone else may succeed."

His voice grew weaker and then he fell silent. About thirty minutes later, he tried to speak again but couldn't. He weakly squeezed my hand, and his eyes closed forever.

349   Margaret, I don't know what to say about the sudden loss of this amazing person. How can I express the depth of my sadness? No words seem to be enough. I'm crying and feeling overwhelmed by disappointment. But I'm on my way to England, where I hope to find some comfort.

Wait, something is interrupting me. What could these sounds mean? It's midnight, and the wind is blowing gently. The crew on deck is barely moving. I hear it again, a voice that sounds human but rougher. It's coming from the cabin where Frankenstein's remains are. I have to get up and check. Good night, my sister.

Oh my goodness! Something unbelievable just happened! I'm still feeling dizzy thinking about it. I'm not sure if I can even describe it, but this story wouldn't be complete without this incredible ending.

350   I went into the cabin where my unfortunate and extraordinary friend's remains were lying. Above him was something that I cannot find the right words to describe; it was huge but looked strange and distorted. As it leaned over the coffin, its face was hidden by long tangled hair. But one of its hands was enormous, and seemed to be the color and texture of a mummy. When it heard me coming, it stopped crying out in sorrow and fear, and quickly moved toward the window. I had never seen a face so terrifying and revolting before. It was disgusting, but also terrifyingly horrifying. I closed my eyes instinctively and tried to remember what I should do in the presence of this monster. I called out for it to stop.

It paused and looked at me in amazement. Then, it turned back to the lifeless body of its creator and seemed to forget I was there. Every expression and movement showed that it was consumed by a wild rage, beyond its control.

"He is also my victim!" it cried out. "His murder completes my crimes. The miserable existence I have lived is coming to an end! Oh, Frankenstein! You were kind and sacrificed yourself for others! What good does it do now for me to ask for your forgiveness? I destroyed you completely by taking away everything you loved. Alas! He is cold and cannot answer me."

351 His voice sounded choked, and my initial instincts to grant my friend's dying wish and destroy his enemy were put on hold by a mix of curiosity and sympathy. I approached this enormous being, too afraid to look at his face. I tried to speak, but I could not. The monster kept on rambling, saying things that didn't make sense. Finally, I gathered the courage to speak to him during a brief pause in his storm of emotions. "Your regret," I said, "is unnecessary now. If you had listened to your conscience and not let yourself unleash such evil, Frankenstein would still be alive."

"And do you think," the monster said, "that I could not feel agony and remorse back then? He," he pointed to the dead body, "he did not suffer as much as I did. Do you think I found pleasure in hearing Clerval's cries of pain? I was meant to feel love and empathy, but when misery forced me into hatred, the change caused me unimaginable torment."

352 "After I killed Clerval, I went back to Switzerland feeling crushed and overwhelmed. I felt sorry for Frankenstein, but that feeling turned into horror. I hated myself. But when I discovered that Frankenstein, the one who brought me into existence and caused me unimaginable suffering, dared to hope for happiness while he piled more misery and despair onto me, I became filled with envy and anger. I wanted revenge more than anything. I remembered my promise and decided to make it happen. I knew that seeking revenge would only bring me more pain, but I couldn't resist the impulse. But when she died! Well, I wasn't sad then. I had numbed myself to all

emotions, giving in completely to my despair. Evil became my purpose. Once I had started down this path, I couldn't turn back. Completing my plan for revenge became an all-consuming obsession. And now it's done; he was my last victim!"

353   At first, I felt sorry when I saw how miserable he looked. But then I remembered what Frankenstein had said about his ability to talk persuasively. And when I saw my friend lying lifeless, I couldn't help but feel angry again. I said to him, "You are a terrible person! It's convenient for you to come here and complain about the devastation you caused. You set fire to a group of buildings, and when they burn down, you sit among the ruins and cry. You are a hypocritical monster! If the person you're mourning was still alive, they would still be your target, your cursed revenge. You don't feel pity; you only grieve because the person you wanted to harm has been taken away from you".

354   "It's not like that, not at all," interrupted the creature. "But I understand that you might think that way based on my actions. I don't expect you to feel sorry for me or understand my suffering. When I first sought understanding, it was because I wanted to share the love of kindness and the happiness that filled me. But now, kindness feels like a distant memory, and happiness has turned into bitterness and despair. So, why would I still seek sympathy? I'm okay with suffering alone for as long as it lasts. When I die, I'm fine with being remembered with disgust and shame. I used to dream of leading a virtuous life, gaining fame, and finding joy. I used to hope that there would be people who could see past my appearance and appreciate the good qualities I had. I had lofty ambitions of honor and devotion. But now, my crimes have reduced me lower than the lowest animal. There is no guilt, no harm, no malice, and no misery that can compare to mine. When I reflect on the horrible list of my wrongdoings, it's hard to believe that I'm the same person who once had beautiful visions of goodness. But it's true; I have become a wicked devil, just like that fallen angel. Yet even that enemy of God

and humanity had friends and companions during his loneliness. I am completely alone."

355   "You, who consider Frankenstein as your friend, seem to know about the bad things I did and the misfortunes he faced because of me. But, in his explanation to you, he couldn't fully capture the months and hours of misery that I endured, wasting away in my powerless anger. Even though I crushed his dreams, I was not satisfied with what I did. I always longed for love and companionship, but I was still rejected. Isn't that unfair? Am I the only one to blame when everyone in the world treated me badly? Why don't you hate Felix, who harshly kicked his friend out? Why don't you despise the country person who wanted to harm the savior of his child? No, these are good and faultless people! I, on the other hand, am miserable and abandoned. I am seen as a useless and unimportant thing, to be rejected, kicked, and trampled on. Even now, I get angry when I think about how unfair all of this was."

356   But it's true that I am a terrible person. I have killed innocent and defenseless people. I have choked the life out of someone who never did me or anyone else any harm. I have caused my creator, who represents all that is good and deserving of love, to suffer greatly. I have relentlessly pursued them until they met their untimely demise. They now lie motionless and lifeless. You despise me, but your hatred cannot compare to the way I feel about myself. I see the hands that committed these terrible acts and I think about the heart that imagined them. I long for the day when I can no longer see those hands and when those terrible thoughts no longer plague my mind.

357   "Don't worry that I'll cause more harm in the future. My task is almost finished. I don't need anyone, including you, to die in order for me to complete my purpose. But I do need to end my own life. I plan to leave your boat on the icy raft that brought me here and travel to the farthest point of the North Pole. There, I will gather wood for a funeral pyre and burn this miserable body to ash. I don't want anyone, especially those with twisted intentions, to use my

remains to create another monster like me. I will die. I won't have to endure the agony that torments me now or suffer from unfulfilled desires. The person who gave me life is already dead, and once I am gone, no one will remember us. I won't see the sun, the stars, or feel the wind on my face any longer. Light, feeling, and senses will all fade away, and that's how I will find my happiness. Years ago, when I first experienced the wonders of this world—when I felt the warmth of summer, heard the rustling of leaves, and the beautiful songs of birds—those things meant everything to me, and I would have cried at the thought of dying. But now, it's the only comfort I have. I am stained by my terrible deeds and consumed by overwhelming guilt. Death is the only way I can find peace."

358 "Goodbye! I am leaving you, and you are the last person I will ever lay eyes on. Goodbye, Frankenstein! If you were still alive and harbored a desire for revenge against me, it would be better satisfied while I am alive rather than in my destruction. Even though you feel you were ruined, my agony surpassed yours. The sharp pain of remorse will continue forever.

"But soon," he said, "I will die, and the things I feel now will no longer be felt. These intense miseries will come to an end. My ashes will be carried into the sea by the wind. My spirit will rest peacefully, and if it thinks, it will not surely think like this. Goodbye."

As he said this, he jumped out of the cabin window onto the ice-raft that was near the ship. He was quickly carried away by the waves and disappeared into the darkness and distance.

THE END.